JUST STUPID!

Is this the right book for you?
Take the STUPID TEST and find out.

YES NO

❑ ❑ Do you push doors marked PULL and pull doors marked PUSH?

❑ ❑ Do you worry about getting sucked into the top of an escalator?

❑ ❑ Do you believe a boogeyman hides under your bed?

❑ ❑ Do you automatically turn around when somebody yells, "Hey, Stupid!"?

❑ ❑ Do you think that being able to stuff your mouth full of marshmallows is a sign of superior intelligence?

SCORE: Give yourself one point for each YES answer.

3–5 You are extremel[illegible]
You will love thi[illegible]

1–2 You are fairly st[illegible]
You will love thi[illegible]

0 You think you're really smart, but deep down you're as stupid as the rest of us.
You will love this book.

Also by Andy Griffiths

Just Annoying!
Just Joking!
The Day My Butt Went Psycho!
Zombie Butts from Uranus!

ANDY GRIFFITHS

JUST Stupid!

Scholastic Inc.

New York Toronto London Auckland Sydney
Mexico City New Delhi Hong Kong Buenos Aires

ISBN 0-439-42474-7

12 11 10 9 8 7 6 5 4 3 2 1 4 5 6 7 8 9/0

Printed in the U.S.A. 40
First Scholastic printing, July 2004

JUST Stupid!

POP!

CONTENTS

We do hope you have enjoyed the CONTENTS PAGE. feel free to return at any time for another read.

This page would be BLANK if I were not here telling you that this page would be BLANK if I were not here telling you that this page would be BLANK if I

BURSTING

I'm in the supermarket trying to remember what groceries Mom wanted me to pick up, but I can't think. I can't breathe. I can't do anything. I'm bursting. And I don't mean bursting. I mean BURSTING!

I've got to find a toilet. Fast. Then I can come back and think about the shopping with a clear head. Or not so much a clear head as an empty bladder.

I haven't got a second to lose. I run down the aisle and skid around the corner.

WHAM!

Straight into an old guy with a walker. He staggers forward and crashes into a stack of cans. They go rolling all over the floor. The old man is lying in the middle of them.

"Well, don't just stand there," he says. "Help me up!"

I reach down, take hold of his hand, and pull him to his feet. Luckily, he's not very heavy. I stand his walker up for him. He's muttering words I don't understand.

The store manager appears. I can tell he's the store manager because his pants are too tight. Plus he's wearing a badge that says STORE MANAGER.

"What happened?" he says.

Before I can say anything, the old man answers.

"This silly young boy knocked me over. It wouldn't have happened in my day. When I was young, we respected our elders."

"It was an accident!" I say.

"Were you running?" says the store manager.

"Yes," I say, "but I'm . . ."

"There's no excuse," he says. "I think you owe this gentleman an apology. Then you can pick up all the cans."

"But I'm bursting!"

"You should have thought about that before you started knocking people over and destroying my displays," he says.

I get the feeling that I'm going to get out of

here quicker if I just do what he says. I turn to the old man.

"I'm sorry," I say. "I shouldn't have been running, and I hope you're not hurt."

He shrugs and mutters something else that I can't understand. I start picking up the cans. I can't believe how far they've rolled. Some have rolled at least two or three aisles away. And the store manager makes me pick up every last one.

By the time I've finished, I'm seriously bursting.

But I know better than to run out of the store. This time, I just walk very quickly.

I get outside the supermarket and into the main shopping mall. I'm looking for a sign pointing to the toilet. I can't see one.

There is a man selling pencils outside the supermarket.

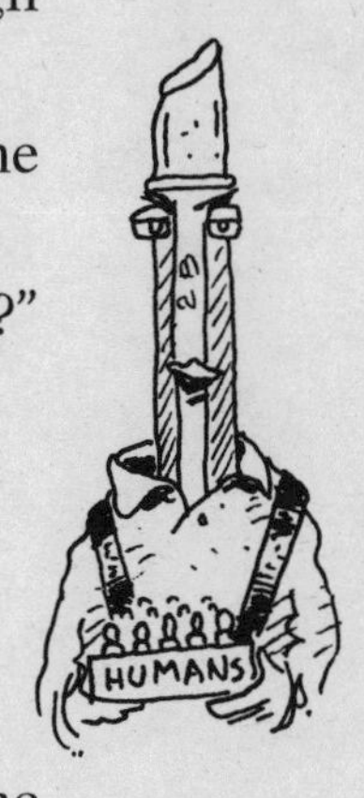

"Excuse me," he says. "Want to buy a pencil?"

"No, thanks," I say.

"They're cheap — twenty cents each."

"No, thank you," I say.

"Just one," he says. "One lousy pencil!"

"I haven't got time!" I say.

"You could have bought one by now," he says.

For information on HOW TO WIN A LIFETIME'S SUPPLY OF FREEZER BAGS, turn to Page 186. →

"How many times do I have to say it?" I say. "I don't want — or need — a pencil. What I need is a toilet. I'm bursting!"

His shoulders drop. He sighs heavily. He looks like he's going to cry. If he's trying to make me feel bad, he's succeeding.

"Okay," I say, fumbling for change. "I'll buy a pencil."

I can't find twenty cents. All I can find is a dollar.

"Have you got change?" I say.

"No," he says. "You're the first one to buy a pencil today."

"Keep the change then," I say.

"No, that wouldn't be right," he says. "I'm not looking for charity."

"Fine," I say, "give me five pencils!"

He counts the pencils out really slowly, one by one. He makes a mistake and has to start again. I'm shifting from foot to foot.

Finally, he hands me the pencils.

"Have a great day," he says.

"I will if I don't burst," I say. I run off before he figures out another way to waste my time.

I'm running as fast as I can, but I'm not sure where to. I have no idea where the toilets are. This shopping mall is too big. There are too

NOT TURN HIS PAGE.

many levels. Too many people getting in my way. I want to scream.

I trip and stumble. I look down. My shoelaces have come undone. I hate my shoelaces. It doesn't matter how well I tie them, they just keep coming undone. I can't ignore them, either, because they're extra-long laces. Now I have to stop and waste valuable toilet-searching seconds retying them.

SHOPPING HINTS.

- Go into the butcher's shop.
- Ask them if they sell meat.
- Ask them how much it is.
- Do they have any steak?
- Does it come with fries?
- Can you have it in a cone?

I kneel down. It's not easy. It's putting pressure on a part of my body that's already under too much strain. I grab the laces and pull them tight. I loop them around each other. Then I loop the loops together and pull them tight as well. That should hold it. At least for a little while. I do the other shoe. I try to stand up. It hurts even more than kneeling down. I don't have much time.

Suddenly, hanging overhead, I find the sign I've been looking for. A picture of a man, a woman, a wheelchair, and an arrow pointing to the left. I turn and sprint down a little corridor. I can see the toilets up ahead of me.

Oh no. I don't believe it. There's a yellow plastic pyramid outside the door.

Closed for cleaning!

Of all the times to clean a toilet, why now? Why not at night when there's nobody here?

Should I try to find another toilet or just wait?

I'll wait.

But I'm bursting.

I can't wait.

But I can't not wait.

I have to go. Right now.

Why does life have to be so difficult?

Hang on! The handicapped toilet is not closed.

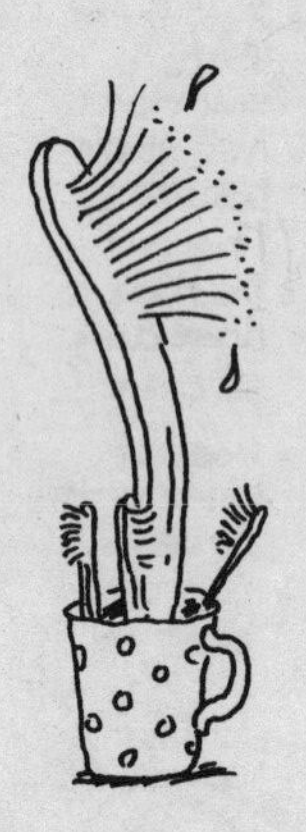

Can you go to jail for using a handicapped person's toilet when you're not really handicapped? Surely not. I'm sure nobody would mind.

I hobble up to the door and push it open. It's vacant. I want to go in but something is stopping me. It would be so easy to just slip in here, and yet, so wrong.

If I get away with using this toilet, who's to say where or when it will stop? I could be taking the first step toward a life of crime. Today the handicapped toilet — tomorrow I'll be leaving my bike in the spaces reserved for handicapped drivers and walking up access ramps for the disabled instead of taking the stairs.

I can't do it. I let go of the door. I might be bursting, but I'm not a criminal.

"Hey!" yells a voice. "You can't use that toilet! You're not handicapped!"

I turn around. Oh no. It's the old guy with the walker. He's hobbling up the corridor toward me.

"I'm not going to use it," I say, backing away from the door.

"Then why did you have the door open?" he says.

"Well, I *was* going to use it, but . . ."

"Aha! I thought so," he says. "Tearing around the supermarket and knocking people over. Using the handicapped people's toilets and stopping the truly handicapped from using them. You're a menace to society. I'm going to call a security guard!"

"No!" I say. "I'm not a menace — I'm just bursting!"

But the old man is not listening.

"Help! Guards! Arrest this boy!"

He's crazy. I've got to get out of here. He's creating such a racket, you'd think he was being murdered or something.

I run down the corridor and back into the

shopping mall. I'm not sure where I'm going. I need to find a location map.

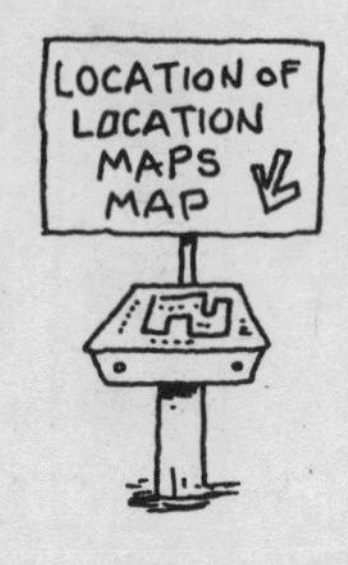

I pass a shop with an enormous poster of a river in the front window. It's an ad for a video called "Great Rivers of the World." If I don't find a toilet fast, there'll be one more great river in the world. Right here in the shopping mall.

I can't hold out much longer. I can hear splashing. Uh-oh. I look down.

No, it's not coming from me. That's a relief. Well, sort of.

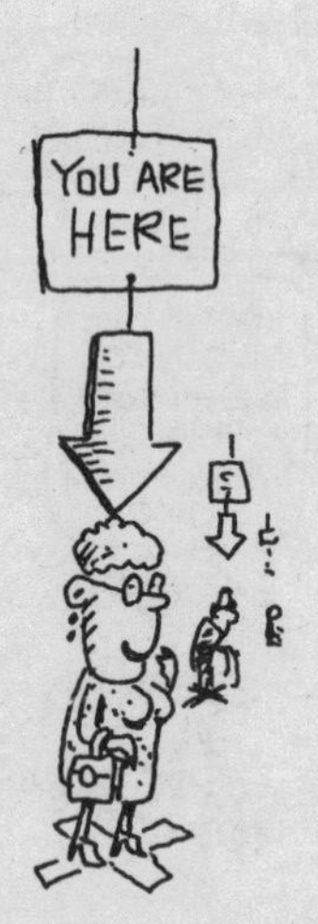

I look around. It's coming from the indoor fountain. There are about fifty thousand jets spraying water in every direction. The sound of all that water is excruciating, but it does give me an idea. Maybe I could go in the fountain. I could get in, stand in the middle, and pretend to be a statue. I could squirt water out of my mouth at the same time. Nobody would even realize.

But hang on! In front of the fountain is a map of the shopping mall. Fantastic!

I hobble over to the map. Hmmm. There are about half a million shops spread across three levels. So there are actually three maps. Lower, middle, and upper, with letters and numbers

around the border of each one. It's very complicated.

And the sound of all that splashing is not making it any easier to concentrate. Whose idea was it to put a fountain inside a shopping mall, anyway? I'd like to find that person and tell them they made a big mistake. And I'd like to find the person who made the shopping mall. I think they made the biggest mistake of all.

This shopping mall is way too big. I mean, do we really need button shops? Or shops that sell nothing except stuff made out of wicker? And as if there aren't already more than enough shops to buy gifts in, some genius comes up with the idea of a gift shop. As far as I'm concerned, the only thing more stupid than a gift shop is a shop that sells nothing but cat toys — and there's one of those here as well.

It doesn't help that the front of the map is suddenly smeared with water. I turn around. Two little kids are squirting each other with water pistols.

"Quit it!" I say.

They don't reply. They just squirt me. Right in the front of my pants.

There's a guy wearing a rainbow-colored shirt standing next to me. He looks like a hippie but I'll ask him anyway. That's how desperate I am.

"Excuse me," I say.

He turns toward me. His eyes are half closed. He looks like he hasn't slept for about three weeks.

"Can you help me find the toilet?" I say.

"Looks like it's a bit late," he says in a slow voice.

"What do you mean?" I say.

He points to the front of my pants.

"That's not what you think it is," I say. "But it will be if you don't help me find the toilet."

"Chill out, man," says the hippie. He turns back to the map and studies it carefully. "Says here the toilets are at M sixteen on level two."

"What level are we on now?" I say.

"Ummm, level three," he says, squinting at the map. "No, hang on . . . level one . . . oops — make that level four."

"Level four?" I say. "There's no such level!"

"Hey, man," says the hippie, "open your mind. There are many levels. More levels than you ever dreamed of."

"Are you insane?" I say.

"Relax," he says. "Take it easy."

"I can't!" I yell. "I'm bursting! I've got to get to a toilet! Quick!"

"No, man, you're missing the point," he says. "The destination's not important. The journey is where it's at."

"Not when you're bursting it's not," I say.

I can't stand still any longer. I start running. I see an escalator going up. I jump on.

I don't believe it. It's almost too good to be true. At the top of the escalator is a sign. A man, a woman, and a wheelchair.

I bound up the last few steps and leap off the escalator. Suddenly, my leg is jerked backward.

I look behind me.

My shoelace is caught in the top of the escalator! I try to pull my foot away, but I can't. The lace is in too deep.

I have to unlace my shoe.

I bend down and poke my finger in between the tongue and the lace. But I can't pull the lace out because the escalator has grabbed the other end of it as well. My finger is trapped.

The laces are being pulled tighter and tighter. My finger is turning bright red. It's throbbing.

Great! Now I'm bursting *and* I've got my shoelace stuck in an escalator *and* my finger stuck in my shoe.

I have to get my shoe off. I don't care about my shoe. All I care about is . . . well, you know what I care about.

I put the index finger of my other hand into the back of my shoe to try to pry my heel out.

Oh no.

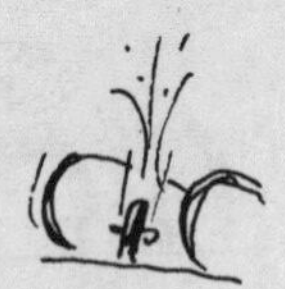

I don't believe it.

I can't get my finger out of the back of the shoe. The shoe is getting tighter. And tighter. And tighter.

The escalator is sucking. And sucking. And sucking.

There's nothing I can do, apart from chew my foot off. That's it! Chewing! Only I don't have to chew through my ankle . . . just my shoelace.

I bend right down. I'm trying to get close enough to the lace to take a good bite. All of a sudden my scalp starts burning. My hair is caught in the escalator!

This is like the most impossible and painful game of Twister ever. I'm bent over double, looking upside down through my legs.

Oh no.

The old man is coming up the escalator. He's got his walker held out in front of him. He's coming right for me.

He hits me fair and square in the butt.

I tumble forward. The shoelace has snapped and a huge chunk of my hair has been ripped out, but I don't care. I'm free!

"Now we're even!" shouts the old man.

"No we're not," I say, scrambling to my feet, "because you just did me a big favor!"

He looks dumbfounded.

I start running.

I'm almost there. Only a few more feet. Something is stabbing me in the leg. What is that? I put my hand into my pocket.

Aaaggh! Something jabs me in the thumb. It's those stupid pencils. They're too sharp. Like little spears. They could do me a serious injury in there. As I pull them out of my pocket, they spill onto the ground in front of me. Uh-oh. Bad move. I'm going too fast to stop. I slip on them and fall backward. I whack my head.

Next thing I know, I'm being shaken awake. I open my eyes. A fireman is kneeling beside me. The corridor is filled with smoke, and I can hear sirens.

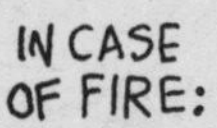

TAKE PROPER PRECAUTIONS

AVOID PANIC

ASSIST OTHERS

PADDLE CALMLY TO THE EXITS

"Wake up!" says the fireman. "Are you okay?"

"What?" I say. "What's happening?"

He lifts me to my feet. I slip on a pencil and fall back down.

"You have to get out of here," he says. "Fire!"

He lifts me up again and starts steering me toward the exit. Away from the toilet!

I try to head back toward the toilet but he grabs me.

"Wrong way," he says, pointing toward the exit. "That way."

"But I have to use the toilet," I say. "I'm bursting!"

"You'll have to wait," says the fireman. "It's not safe! You have to get out of the building."

"Not safe?!" I say. "If I don't get to the toilet soon, nobody will be safe. This shopping mall will be flooded!"

But he's not listening. He's escorting me to the exit.

Outside, there are four fire trucks in a row. The firemen are spraying enormous arcs of water onto the building. It might be helping to extinguish the fire, but it's definitely not helping me.

I overhear the fire chief talking on his walkie-talkie.

"All we know is that the fire appears to have started in one of the escalators," he says. "Some foreign material may have got in there and shorted the system. Until we can put out the fire, we can't be sure. But to do that, we're going to need backup units . . . as many as you've got."

He wipes the sweat off his brow.

Suddenly, I know what I have to do. I can solve my problem and be a hero at the same time.

"Excuse me," I say, "you're not going to need those backup units."

"What are you talking about?" he says.

"You've got me," I say.

"Huh?"

"Watch this!" I say.

I go as close to the burning building as I can. I take aim.

Ahhhhhhhhhhhhhhhh. Relief! Beautiful relief. The fire is powerless against me. It disappears in clouds of steam. People are gathered around and applauding. The supermarket manager is there. And the pencil seller. And the hippie. Even the old man. Cheering. Chanting my

name. I don't know how they know my name, but I don't care about that right now. All I care about is how good this feels. And how warm. It's so warm.

I roll over and snuggle down deeper into my blankets. My blankets? What are my blankets doing here? And why am I wearing pajamas?

I blink a few times. I rub my eyes.

There's no shopping mall. There are no fire trucks. No people.

I'm in my bedroom. In my bed. Wrapped in my blankets. Putting out a fire. Only there's no fire, either.

I hate that.

I mean it.

expel me!

DANGER: Beware the smiling Principal.

It's the first day back at school.

And if all goes according to plan, it will also be my last.

I'm sitting in the back corner of the classroom. Well, I'm not really sitting. I'm leaning back on the chair, putting all my weight on the back legs, just like we're not supposed to.

And that's not the only rule I'm breaking.

My feet are up on the desk. I'm not wearing any shoes. I'm wearing a cap. My T-shirt is ripped. Plus, it has an offensive slogan on the front. I've got my Walkman on. On the table in front of me is a packet of bubble gum, a spitball shooter, and some freshly chewed spitballs. On the blackboard, I've drawn this crazy-looking stick figure with bugged-out

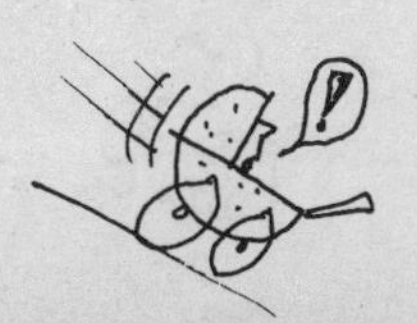

eyes and buckteeth. It's hitting itself over the head with a hammer and saying "Look at me — I'm your stupid new teacher!" And underneath it I've written BY ANDY GRIFFITHS, so that there's no chance anybody else will get the blame.

I figure the new teacher will be like all new teachers. They'll be wanting to show everybody how tough they are. They won't be wanting to fool around with warnings or detentions or phone calls to parents. They'll be looking for a scapegoat to send straight to the principal's office. Well, they won't have to look for long. Here I am — ready and willing.

Danny comes into the room. He looks at me and his mouth falls open.

"Are you crazy?" he finally says. He's obviously having trouble taking in the full extent of my badness.

"No," I say.

"But your feet . . . your T-shirt . . . the spitball shooter . . ." splutters Danny. "Boy, are you going to get it!"

"Good," I say. "I want to get it. I want to be expelled."

"Expelled?" he says.

"I'm sick of school," I say.

“But it’s only the first day back,” he says. “And school hasn’t even started yet. How can you be sick of it?”

“Are you kidding?” I say. “I can’t live like this. Bells, schedules, lessons, rules and regulations — they’re not for me. I had a taste of freedom during summer vacation, and I decided I’m not coming back.”

“But you’re here,” says Danny.

“Only long enough to get myself expelled,” I say. “Then I’m out of school for good.”

“But your parents will just send you somewhere else,” says Danny.

“You don’t get it, Dan, do you?” I say. “If my parents try that, I’ll just get myself expelled from there as well.”

Danny smiles.

“You think it’s that easy?” he says.

“Of course it is,” I say. “What could be easier? It’s not like there’s any shortage of rules to break.”

“You’re not wrong there,” says Danny, nodding.

“And when you think about it,” I say, “how hard is it to break a rule?”

“It’s not hard,” says Danny, now shaking his head. “It’s not hard at all.”

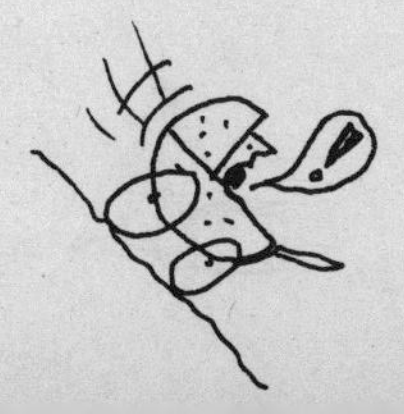

"Better to die on your feet than live on your knees," I say.

"Yeah," says Danny, "you're right. Because living on your knees would be really uncomfortable. Your pants would wear out and your knees would get all scabby, and it would take ages to get anywhere. . . ."

"We *are* living on our knees, Dan," I say. "But not me. Not any longer. I'm walking out of here."

Danny looks at me, his eyes shining.

"Can I get expelled with you?" he says.

"Sure," I say. "Between us, we can break twice as many rules as I could on my own. We'll be out of here in no time."

"All right!" says Danny.

"It's a deal!" I say, holding out my hand. "Give me the secret handshake."

"What is it again?" says Danny, bending over and putting his hand through his leg. "Is this right?"

"No, Dan," I say, "that's the old one. Honestly, what's the point of having a secret handshake if you can never remember it?"

"Well it's been a while," he says, "what with summer vacation and everything."

I'm about to show him, when a woman

comes into the room. She must be our new teacher.

"Quick — get into position," I say. "Don't worry about the handshake. And don't forget to take your shoes off."

I lean back on my chair. The new teacher is holding an old-fashioned projector and a small yellow slide box.

"Good morning," she says. "My name is Ms. Livingstone. Sorry I'm a little late. I had a bit of trouble finding the room. I flew in very late last night, and I didn't get much sleep. I was supposed to arrive a few weeks ago, but the yacht I was sailing was destroyed by a tsunami in the middle of the Pacific Ocean. I was marooned on a tiny island for many days before the rescue helicopters saw my smoke signals. I was beginning to give up hope that they would find me before the school year started. But as you can see, here I am, safe and sound — just a little tired."

Excited murmuring breaks out all around the room.

I think they actually believe her!

I look at Danny and roll my eyes.

"As if!" I say.

She probably just slept in. Just like I'll be

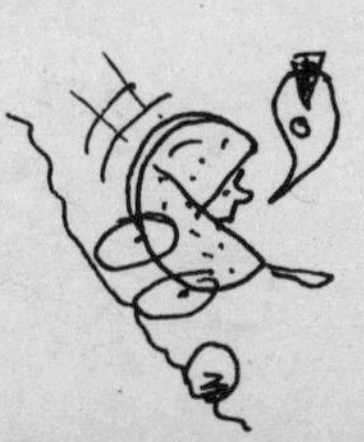

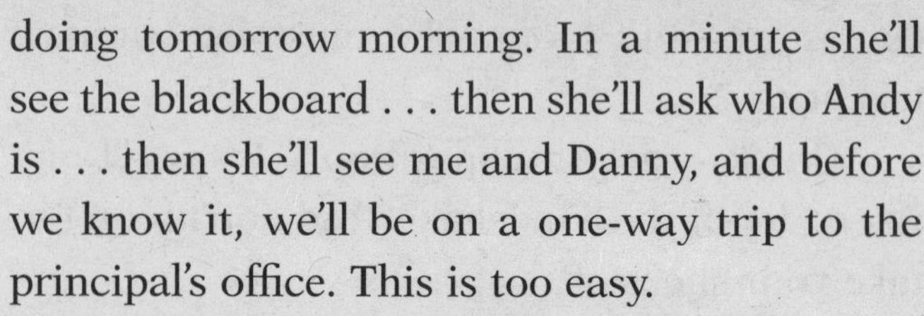

doing tomorrow morning. In a minute she'll see the blackboard . . . then she'll ask who Andy is . . . then she'll see me and Danny, and before we know it, we'll be on a one-way trip to the principal's office. This is too easy.

She still hasn't noticed me — too busy fussing with the stuff on her desk. She hasn't seen the blackboard. I have to get her to turn around.

"Would you like me to clean the blackboard for you?" I say.

"Yes, thank you," she says without looking at it — or me.

"Okay," I say, stomping up the aisle as loudly as I can and swinging my arms in the stupidest and most attention-getting walk I can manage.

As I'm walking, I accidentally knock Lisa Mackney's folder off her table. It goes flying, hits the floor, and the pages spill out everywhere. Lisa stares at me. I wish this had happened to anybody's folder but Lisa's.

"I'm sorry, Lisa," I whisper.

I get down on my knees and start gathering up the paper. I push it all into the folder as neatly as I can.

"That's really nice of you to help pick all

that up," says Ms. Livingstone. "You must be quite a gentleman."

"But it was me who knocked it off in the first place," I say.

"We all make mistakes," she says.

"But I did it on purpose," I say.

She laughs.

"I can't believe that somebody as helpful as you would do a thing like that," she says. "And even if you did, I'm sure you had a very good reason for it."

"No, I didn't," I say. "I did it because I'm bad and evil and I deserve to be sent straight to the principal's office."

Ms. Livingstone laughs again. She thinks I'm joking.

"Look at the board if you don't believe me," I say.

Ms. Livingstone looks at the board.

"That's very amusing," she says. "Who is it supposed to be?"

"It's you!" I say.

"Me?" she says. "It doesn't look anything like me."

She picks up a piece of chalk and, with just a few quick lines and squiggles, draws a perfect caricature of herself.

TO BE REALLY MEAN, YOU MUST:

Head butt lampposts.

PUSH OVER INTERNATIONAL ICONS.

Refuse to eat your Broccoli.

"That's me," she says.

The whole class is laughing. Even me.

Then she draws another figure with a really crazy face. Boy, is it ugly and stupid-looking. It's much better than the one I drew.

"And that's you," she says.

The class laughs even harder. I stop laughing.

"So you're not angry?" I say.

"Angry?" she says. "Of course not. I'm flattered that you've gone to so much trouble to welcome me."

"Well," I say, "aren't you at least going to tell me off for wearing my cap inside?"

"No," she says, "I find the fluorescent light very harsh myself. I don't blame you."

I'm thrusting out my chest.

"What about my T-shirt?" I ask.

"What about it?" she says.

"It's got an offensive slogan on it," I say.

Ms. Livingstone laughs.

"Who would be offended by that?" she says.

"Anybody who reads it, I guess," I say.

"Well, not necessarily," she says. "Whether something is offensive is very much in the eye of the beholder. For example, in our culture,

burping is considered offensive — but in some cultures, not to burp after a meal is a horrible insult to the host. Once when I was traveling in a foreign land I was invited to dine with a king. It was a magnificent feast, but afterward I was almost put to death because I was unable to show my appreciation by burping."

The class gasps.

"It wasn't until he had his knife at my throat," she continues, "that I was able to reach deep within myself and produce the burp that saved my life. After three months there, I became quite an expert."

She gulps some air and lets out the most earsplitting burp I've ever heard. It's even louder than one of Danny's.

The whole class applauds. But not me. I can fake-burp anytime I feel like it. It's no big deal.

I stomp back to my desk.

There must be some way to annoy her. I know — I'll ask some stupid questions.

"Excuse me, Ms. Livingstone," I say without putting my hand up.

"Yes?"

"Have you ever been to Germany?"

"Yes," she says, "I have."

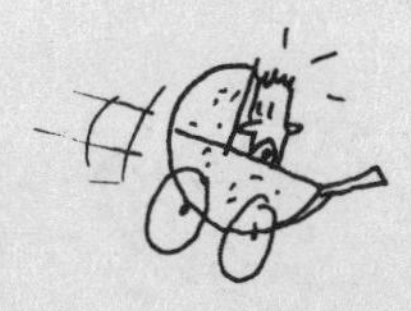

"Do people get sick a lot in Germany?"

"No more than other places, I expect," she says. "Why do you ask?"

"I just thought with all the *germs* and everything . . ."

The class erupts with laughter.

One to me.

Ms. Livingstone runs her hand through her hair.

"Well, that's actually a very interesting question you've raised, Andy," she says. "Standards of health vary all over the world. For instance, when I was living with the Eskimos, I noticed that . . ."

Danny leans forward.

"You lived with Eskimos?" he says. "In an igloo?"

"Oh, yes," she says. "I was part of an expedition searching for the Abominable Snowman."

The whole class is silent while she explains. One to her.

"Dan," I say. "Dan!"

But he can't hear me. He's too involved in Ms. Livingstone's story. To tell you the truth, it is quite interesting. Especially the stuff about falling into the crevasse and trying to light a fire with only one match and a handful of wet

wood — but that's not the point. We want to be expelled! Or at least I do. Danny can stay here if he wants. I've got things to do, places to be. I'm not sure what they are yet, but I'll think of something.

I might as well stop beating around the bush.

"Ms. Livingstone?" I say.

"Yes, Andy?"

"Can I be expelled?"

"I'm sorry, Andy, but I don't have the power to do that. That's a matter for the principal."

"Can you send me to him?" I say.

"But why?" she says. "What have you done wrong? What rules have you broken?"

"What rules *haven't* I broken!" I say, getting out my school notebook. I start reading: "'No leaning back on chairs. No feet on tables. No hats inside. No offensive slogans on clothing. No eating in class. Show respect to teachers. Show respect to fellow students and their property. No Walkmans. No banging. No tapping. No spitballs.' I've broken every rule there is, and it's not even recess!"

Ms. Livingstone stands there thinking. She's got to send me to the principal's office now. She has no choice.

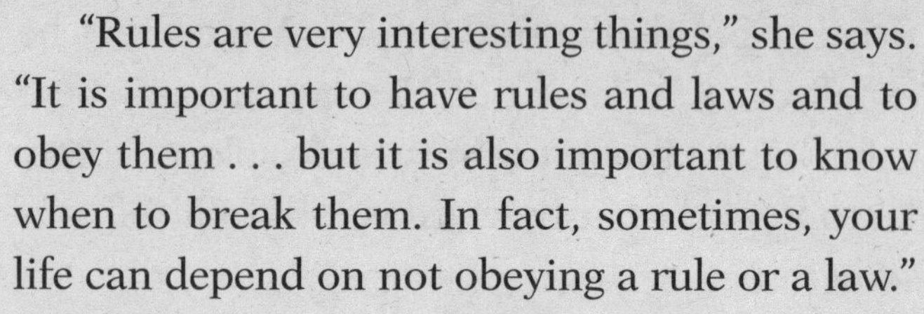

"Rules are very interesting things," she says. "It is important to have rules and laws and to obey them . . . but it is also important to know when to break them. In fact, sometimes, your life can depend on not obeying a rule or a law."

Uh-oh, here we go again.

"For instance," she continues, "in most societies, there are laws against cannibalism, and yet when the light airplane my husband and I were piloting crashed in the Andes and I was stranded for three months without food, I had to decide whether I was going to observe that law and face certain death, or break the law in order to survive."

Ms. Livingstone pauses. Everybody is listening now. Even me.

"You had to eat your husband?" I say.

She stares wistfully into the distance. Tears form in the corners of her eyes. She brushes them away.

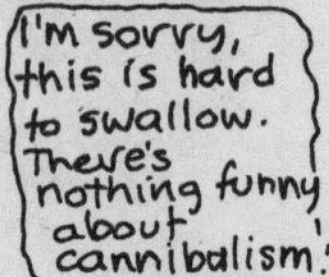

"Perhaps now is not the right time to talk about it," she says. "All I'm saying is that sometimes rules have to be broken."

I check the fingers on her left hand. She's wearing a wedding ring. What a phony. I bet she didn't really eat her husband. I bet she had a secret stash of granola bars or something and

she's just pretending that she ate her husband. She's a fake.

"I thought this morning that I might introduce myself by showing you some slides of my most recent travels," she says. "Can somebody help me to set up the projector and the screen?"

"I will!" says Danny. He practically leaps out of his seat and runs to the closet to get the screen out. Definitely not the sort of behavior that's going to get him expelled.

While he sets up the screen, I lean back on my chair, turn up my Walkman full blast, drum on the table with my hands, and sing the guitar solos at the top of my voice.

Ms. Livingstone doesn't kick me out though. She's saying something to the class. She points at me. They all look across and laugh. Even Lisa. I don't know what Ms. Livingstone said, but I don't think they're laughing with me anymore. They're laughing at me. Another one to her.

She turns the lights out and shows a slide of herself rowing a canoe down a river. On either side of the river is thick jungle.

I pick up my spitball shooter. The thing I really like about slide shows is that they give you a chance to practice precision spitball shoot-

ing. You only get a little bit of time to hit each target before the next slide appears. I take a deep breath and aim my shooter at Ms. Livingstone's pith helmet.

Darn. Too hard. I blew the shooter right out of my hand. It landed up near the front of the room.

I get out of my seat and walk down the aisle to retrieve it.

Suddenly, there's an enormous crash. I've tripped over the projector cord and knocked the slide projector off the table.

Silence.

Ms. Livingstone turns the lights on. She stares at me.

"Please don't feel bad, Andy," she says. "It's time for a new projector, anyway. That's just the excuse I needed to update. I've always wanted one with a remote-control wheel, but while the other projector still worked, I just couldn't justify the expense."

I pick up my spitball shooter and go back to my desk. Looks like getting sent to the principal's office is going to be harder than I thought. I've still got one last weapon though. Blood capsules!

I take two out of my pocket.

"Danny," I say, "pretend to punch me in the mouth."

"Punch you in the mouth?" says Danny. "But why? You're my best friend."

"No, don't really do it," I say. "Just pretend."

"Why?" he says.

"So we get into trouble for fighting. I'm going to bite down on some blood capsules and make it look really bad."

"But I'm not sure I want to get expelled anymore," says Danny.

"What about our deal?" I say.

"But our new teacher is just so cool," he says. "She's so interesting."

"I pity you," I say. "She's not interesting. She's a fake. A phony. She hasn't even eaten her husband."

"How do you know?" says Danny.

"Because she's wearing a wedding ring for a start," I say.

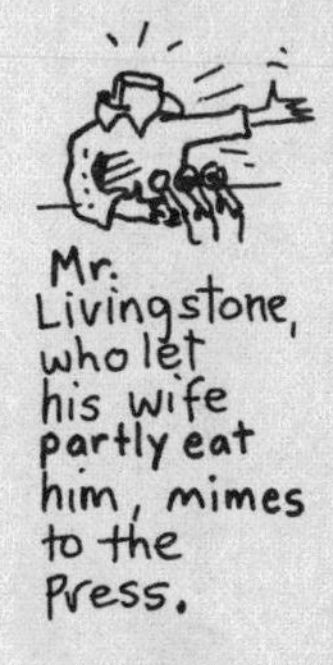

"Maybe she only ate a bit of him and then they were rescued," says Danny.

"What — she ate part of him while he was still alive?" I say.

"Yes," says Danny. "Maybe they just ate his toes or something he didn't really need."

"Suit yourself, Dan," I say. "Believe what

you want — but if you don't want to get expelled, I'll just tell her that you hit me because I provoked you."

"Okay," says Danny. "If you insist."

"I insist," I say.

WHAM!

Danny punches me in the jaw. Hard. I fall to the floor.

"I said to *pretend* to hit me, you moron," I mumble.

"Sorry," he says. "I was trying to make it look real."

I bite down on the capsules. They've got an awful taste. But I can feel the fake blood flowing out of my mouth and down my neck. I roll around, groaning.

"AAAAGGGHHHH . . ." I say. "Aaaagggghhhhh . . ."

Ms. Livingstone comes over and looks down at me.

She shakes her head.

"You're not really hurt, are you, Andy?" she says.

"Yes, I am," I say. "Danny hit me. But it was all my fault. I asked for it, and if anybody should be sent to the principal's office, I think it should be me."

Ms. Livingstone leans down and sniffs my breath.

"Blood capsules," she says, screwing up her face. "There's no mistaking that smell."

She is sharp. I'll give her that. "They're mine," I say. "And I don't blame you for being angry. They are against the rules."

"No, I'm not angry," she says. "I'd just hoped never to see another blood capsule as long as I lived. When I worked as a stunt double for Natasha Teasedale, I had to chew about fifty a day."

"You worked as a stunt double for Natasha Teasedale?" I say. "Which movie?"

"All of them," says Ms. Livingstone.

"Wow," I say. Oops. I didn't mean to say that. I just meant to think it. "I mean, sure you were a stunt double . . . sure, sure."

"It's true," she says. "I grew up in a circus, and then I got into martial arts. I was spotted by Natasha Teasedale's director at a tae kwon do exhibition in Tokyo, and that's how I got into the movies. Falling out of buildings, fighting wild tigers, jumping out of speeding cars . . . you name it, I've done it."

That's amazing. I'd love to stay around and hear more about her movie career, and espe-

cially about working with Natasha Teasedale, but I can't. I have to get expelled. I don't want to spend my life sitting around listening to stories about somebody else's adventures — I want to get out there and have my own.

"That's all very interesting, I'm sure," I say, "but the classroom is no place for stunt work. You should punish me."

"Stunt work?" she guffaws. "You call *that* stunt work? I'll show you stunt work."

She climbs onto my table. "Andy," she says, "get up here!"

"Me?" I say. "Up there?"

She nods. She's serious. She means business.

I climb up on the table. That's another rule broken.

"Okay," she says. "Now punch me."

"You mean pretend to punch you?" I say.

"No," she says. "I mean really punch me."

Punch a teacher? That's guaranteed to get me expelled. And not only expelled, either. I'm a pretty hard hitter. I could really hurt her. I could end up in jail. I'd rather stay in school.

"I don't think I should do this, Ms. Livingstone," I say.

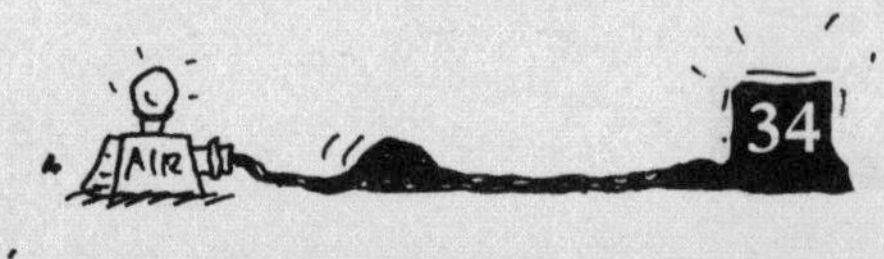

"Come on!" she says, pointing to her chin. "Hit me."

"Okay." I shrug. "You asked for it."

I swing at her chin. But before my fist can connect with her face, she cracks her head back, teeters on the edge of the table for a moment, wobbles, and then, without warning, does a back flip and crashes onto the floor.

The class cheers.

"Now jump down and strangle me!" she says.

"But, Ms. Livingstone," I say.

"Just do it!" she says.

I jump down. I put my hands around her neck. But I don't even get to squeeze it before she lets out a bloodcurdling scream and begins writhing and gasping as if I'm really strangling her. It is very realistic. Not that I've ever strangled anybody, but I'm sure this is what they'd look like if I did.

The door opens and the principal walks in.

I'm gone now.

He looks at the scene — the blackboard graffiti, the broken projector, Ms. Livingstone struggling on the floor, and the worst thing of all, me sitting on top of her, my hands around her throat.

Megan, be Careful with the electric pencil sharpener.
Don't worry Ms., I've used it lots of times.
OH NO, Megan.

"What is the meaning of all this?" he bellows.

I scramble to my feet.

Ms. Livingstone stops her act and gets up.

"Oh, hello, Mr. Stanley," she says. "I was just showing the children some of the tricks of the stunt trade."

The principal nods.

"Oh," he says. "That's all right. I thought something was wrong."

"No, everything's fine," she says. "We've covered falling backward off a table, and now Andy is helping me to demonstrate strangulation."

"I'm very pleased to hear it," he says. "However, I've always felt, and this is just my opinion, that strangulation can be more convincingly simulated if the victim doesn't make any sound. It should all be suggested by the movement of the limbs. Here, let me show you."

He gets down on the floor, on his back, and starts waving his arms and kicking his legs in the air — like a dying fly.

I can't believe what's happening here. For the first time in my life, I am actually learning something interesting and useful at school.

I can't get expelled now. Not until the stunt lesson is over, anyway. And then I want to find

out exactly what happened to Ms. Livingstone in the Andes. And what it was like growing up in a circus. And I've got a million questions to ask about Natasha Teasedale.

I think I'll get expelled next week instead.

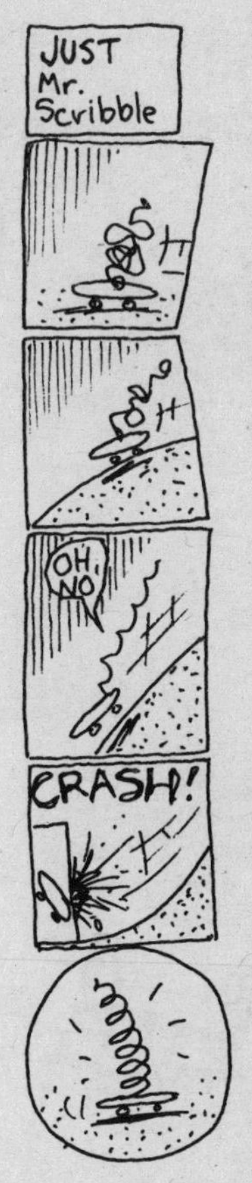

Boogeyboy

I'm cramped.

I'm cold.

I can hardly breathe.

I've been lying underneath my sister's bed for more than an hour now. Where is she? The clock near the front door has just chimed midnight, and she told Mom and Dad she would be home by eleven.

It's not exactly a lot of fun down here.

The bed is really low. Every time I take a breath, my chest presses against the bottom of the bed. I can't even turn my head without scraping my nose.

So why am I here?

I'll tell you why.

Revenge.

I'm doing it to pay Jen back for laughing at me because I wet my bed. Not that I really did wet my bed — well, I did, but it happened because I was trying to put out a fire . . . but it's kind of hard to explain the difference to people like Jen. Especially when they're rolling around on the floor laughing at you.

Well, two can play that game. Jen might not have wet her bed recently, but she is still scared of the boogeyman. I know this because I overheard her confessing it to her boyfriend. She's convinced the boogeyman lives under her bed and is just waiting for a chance to grab her leg and pull her under. Well, tonight her nightmare is going to come true. When she comes home, I'm going to reach out and grab her ankle. She'll die.

She's out on a date with Craig Bennett. They've been going out together since the school dance. I can't imagine what she sees in him. He's got no sense of humor. He tried to punch my head in at the dance because I tricked him into thinking I was a girl. How was I to know he'd fall in love with me? Serves him right for being such a sleaze.

For all I know, they probably got home ages ago and have been standing out in the

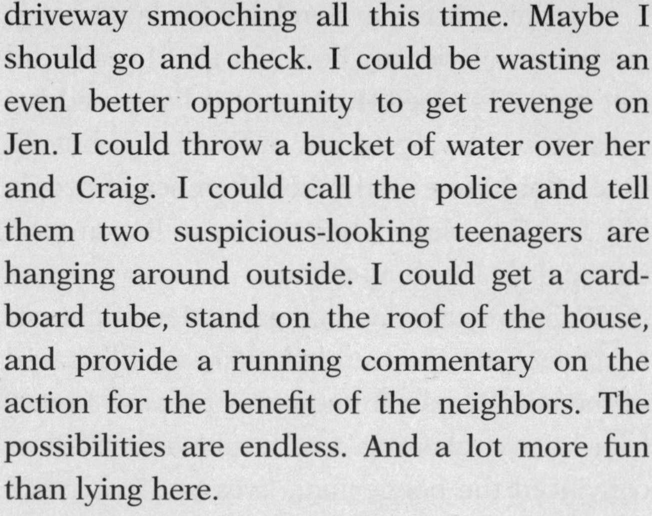

driveway smooching all this time. Maybe I should go and check. I could be wasting an even better opportunity to get revenge on Jen. I could throw a bucket of water over her and Craig. I could call the police and tell them two suspicious-looking teenagers are hanging around outside. I could get a cardboard tube, stand on the roof of the house, and provide a running commentary on the action for the benefit of the neighbors. The possibilities are endless. And a lot more fun than lying here.

I start wriggling out from underneath the bed. Hang on. What's that?

I hear sounds outside. Footsteps coming up the path. I hear the key in the front door.

Just in time!

I wriggle under again. Not long now.

In a moment, Jen will open her bedroom door. She will click on the light. She will approach the bed. I will reach out and grab her ankle. She will scream. I will roar like a monster. She will scream again. I will roar again — but this time not like a monster. I will be roaring with laughter.

I hear whispering. Jen's room is right next to the front door.

THINGS I FOUND UNDER MY BED.
Live old Chewing gum.
Detached Barbie Head (3).
Smurf (without head).
5-week-old decaying sports sock.
Pile of Q-tips (with earwax).

"Would you like to come in?" says Jen.

"Are you sure it's all right?" says Craig.

"Yes, of course I'm sure," says Jen.

"But what about your parents?" says Craig.

"Their bedroom is upstairs," she says. "They won't wake up — and even if they do, I'll just tell them you're borrowing a CD or something."

"What about your stupid little brother?" says Craig. "What if he's still up?"

"Oh don't worry about him," says Jen. "He went to bed hours ago. He's just a child."

"Some child," says Craig. "I should have taught him a lesson while I had the chance. Nobody makes a fool of Craig Bennett and gets away with it."

"He didn't make a fool of you, Craig," says Jen. "He was the one who looked ridiculous."

"Yeah," Craig chuckles. "Those X-Men undies . . . what a loser."

They are both laughing. I don't see what's so funny. The X-Men aren't losers.

"Come on," says Jen. "Just for a minute."

"Well, okay," says Craig. "Just for a minute."

Darn — still more waiting. I hope Craig doesn't stay for long.

They come into the hallway and close the front door very quietly.

Jen flicks her bedroom light on.

"Come in," she says. I hear the door click shut.

Oh no. I don't believe it. She's brought him into her bedroom!

If they find out I'm here, I'll be in serious trouble. They'll think that I'm spying on them. Craig will want to punch my head in again . . . and this time, Jen will probably let him. She'll probably even help him. I've got to get out of here. But I can't. They'll see me.

Jen kicks off her shoes. One comes skidding across the floor and hits me in the left ear. Ouch. I take a deep breath and clench my teeth.

I'm straining my eyes as far around as I can without moving my head to see where they are. I can see their feet. Jen is in the middle of the room. Craig is over near her dressing table.

"Wow," says Craig. "Is this a real crystal ball?"

Jen's got this enormous crystal ball. It's practically as big as a bowling ball. In fact, if you ask me, that's all it's good for. All it needs is three holes drilled in the top and it would be perfect.

"Yes," she says. "I can see the future in it."

"Am I there?" asks Craig.

I see Jen's feet move toward the dressing table.

"Of course you are." Jen laughs. "I had the best night, Craig. You really know how to make a girl feel special."

"That's not hard," says Craig. "You're a pretty special girl, Jen. Here, this is for you."

"Oh, thank you," says Jen. "I love roses. It's beautiful. Just like the ones Dad grows."

"Actually, it is one of your dad's," says Craig. "I picked it on the way in."

"You shouldn't have gone to all that trouble." Jen laughs.

"Nothing's too much trouble for you," says Craig.

I've got to get out of here. Before I throw up. A rose. How corny. What's next? A box of chocolates?

"Ouch!" says Jen. "It pricked me!"

I see the rose hit the floor. It's not far from my head. If she bends down to pick it up she's going to see me. I wriggle as far away from the edge of the bed as I can.

"Are you okay?" says Craig. "Here, let me kiss it and make it better."

THINGS TO DO, TRAPPED UNDER A BED

Compose Poetry

Play imaginary computer games

Dig a tunnel through the wall

Fall asleep

THINGS NOT TO DO HIDING UNDER A BED.

EAT BAKED BEANS.

Try digging a tunnel through the floor.

Use your cell phone.

Relive your great sports moment.

I can see Craig's black leather shoes facing Jen's bare feet in the center of her yin and yang rug. Craig is standing on the white bit. Jen is on the black bit. Their feet are very close. For a few moments there is no sound.

"Oh Craig," says Jen.

"Oh Jen," says Craig.

"Oh brother," I say, only I say it very quietly so that they don't hear me.

Out of the corner of my eye, I see movement.

There's something coming out of the rose.

Something black.

Something hairy.

Something disgusting.

Something with fangs.

And it's heading straight for me.

This is not good. Not only am I trapped underneath my sister's bed while she smooches with a thug who has threatened to punch my head in on at least two occasions, now I've got a killer spider heading straight for my ear hole.

It's not a really big spider or anything, but that makes it even worse. It's the small ones that are really lethal.

What if it gives me one of those bites that

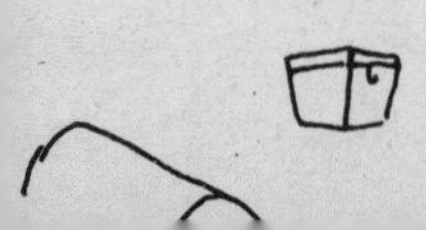

never heals? The kind where your flesh just starts dying and spreads over your whole body until you're practically a zombie.

Or even worse, what if it's pregnant and just wants to paralyze me and lay its eggs in my flesh so that when the babies hatch they've got lots of fresh meat to feed on?

My only hope is that Jen and Craig will see it and deal with it before it reaches me. Look down! Look down!

"Oh Craig," says Jen.

"Oh Jen," says Craig.

I don't think they're going to look down.

The spider is crawling toward me. It's so close, I can see the light glinting off its enormous black fangs. It's coming to get me.

Hang on. Jen and Craig are moving closer to the bed.

Maybe they'll step on it. Come on . . . please . . . please . . .

Craig's feet stop beside the bed.

I can't see the spider anymore. I think he stood on it, but I can't tell for sure.

Hang on.

There it is!

The spider is on the toe of Craig's shoe. It's going to crawl up his leg. Excellent!

Other great PLACES TO HIDE in a bedroom.

In the top drawer.

As hat and Coat stand.

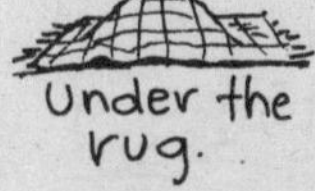

Under the rug.

In the light fixture.

Well, not excellent for Craig, but excellent for me.

All I have to do now is wait. Sooner or later, Craig is going to realize there's a spider on him. He'll freak. Jen will see the spider and go hysterical — she is even more terrified of spiders than she is of the boogeyman. She will scream and run out of the room. Craig will follow, Mom and Dad will wake up, and in all the commotion, I will slip quietly back to my room. Simple.

Suddenly, they sit down on the bed. The bed gets even lower. It buckles under their weight and pushes against my chest. Great. I'm even more cramped than I was before. I wish that spider would hurry up. I'm going to suffocate down here.

I feel an itch on the side of my neck, just below my ear, but I can't scratch it because I'm too squashed. I hate that. It's really itchy and the more I can't scratch the more it itches. I can't stop thinking about it. I need to take my mind off it. I'll do my seven times table. One times seven is seven. Two times seven is fourteen. Three times seven is . . . um . . . um . . . darn this itch! I can't concentrate. I can't even remember

what three times seven is. It's the itchiest itch ever. And it's spreading. Now it's on my cheek.

Hang on. It's not spreading — it's moving. Itches don't move. I don't think it's an itch — I think it's the spider.

Okay. Get a grip. I'm not going to panic. I'm going to stay calm. I can handle this.

I don't know for sure that it's the spider. It could be just a moth. Or an ant. Something harmless.

Whatever it is, I should be able to squash it if I turn my head and press my cheek against my shoulder.

My nose rubs the bottom of the bed as I turn my head.

Not a good idea. Turning my head has made whatever it is move faster.

It's moving up toward my mouth.

I hold my breath. I strain to look down to see what it is. Uh-oh. It's the spider. It looks much bigger close up.

I squeeze my eyes shut and hold my breath. I want to scream, but the spider places a leg across my lips as if to shush me. *This is our secret*, it seems to be saying, *this is just between you and me*.

It draws its furry body across my mouth and pauses. My lips are shut tight.

Okay. This is not good. But I'm not going to panic. I'll be all right if I don't panic. I have to control myself and not alarm the spider.

Maybe I could blow it off.

I part my lips the tiniest amount possible and start to blow. The spider doesn't budge. It lowers and flattens its body like it's trying to hold on.

I need a bigger breath. I breathe in as deeply through my nose as I can and blow harder. But it's still not enough. For all I know, the spider is enjoying this — it must be like standing in front of a warm heater on a cold day.

Suddenly, Jen squeals.

"Stop it, Craig!" She giggles. "That tickles! Stop please, no!"

The bed buckles and thumps down on my chest.

I gasp. Something catches in my throat. I gulp.

Oh no.

I just swallowed the spider!

"Aaaaaggghhhhh!" I scream.

"What's that?" says Craig.

They heard me, but I don't care. All I care about is the spider.

What if it bites me on the inside? That's worse than getting bitten on the outside. The poison will go straight into my bloodstream. I could be dead within minutes.

I'm gagging and coughing, trying to get it out. I'm too young to die.

"It's the boogeyman!" screams Jen. "He's under the bed!"

Craig's face appears beside me.

"More like boogey*boy*," he says. "It's your stupid little brother."

He grabs my arm and drags me out.

But I don't care. He's doing me a favor. I've got to get out of here. I've got to get to a hospital before the poison takes effect. Before the convulsions start.

"Andy!" says Jen.

I try to stand up. It's not easy because I'm so stiff from having been cramped under the bed for so long. Or maybe it's the first sign of the poison setting in. Maybe my whole body will seize up and I won't be able to move!

I stagger to the door.

"Stop him!" says Jen.

Craig strides across the room. He pushes

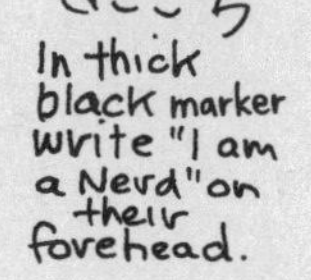

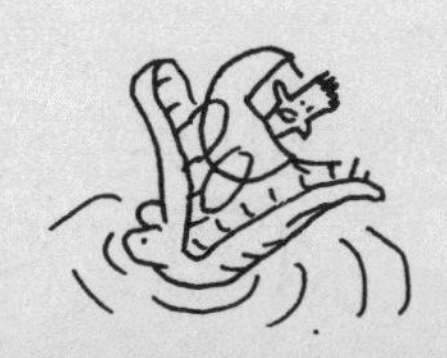

me away from the door and stands with his back against it.

"Not so fast, buddy," he says, rolling up his shirtsleeves. "I think we need to have a little talk."

Jen gets up from the bed and joins Craig at the door.

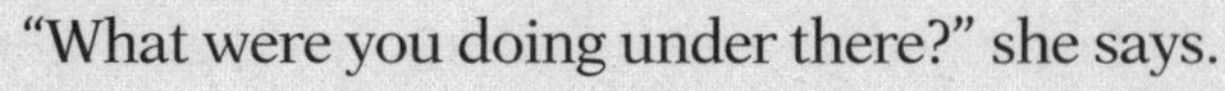

"What were you doing under there?" she says.

"Yeah, you little weirdo!" says Craig. "Explain!"

"I haven't got time to explain," I say. "I have to get to the hospital. It's a matter of life or death."

Craig snorts.

"It's a matter of life or death all right," he says, "but you won't need a hospital by the time I've finished with you. You'll be going straight to the morgue!"

"Yeah, you're in big trouble, Andy," says Jen. "Wait till I tell Mom and Dad!"

"You do that and I'll tell them you got home late and you had Craig in your room!" I say.

"I'll just deny it," says Jen.

"But it's true!" I say.

"I know that and you know that," says Jen. "But who do you think Mom and Dad are going to believe? Me or you?"

She's got a point, but I don't care. I don't care about anything. I'm going to die.

"Please let me go," I beg. "I swear I won't tell anybody anything. Just let me go."

Suddenly I feel the most extraordinary sensation at the back of my throat.

"Are you all right, Andy?" says Jen. "You've turned green!"

"Probably just another one of his dumb tricks," says Craig.

"No," says Jen. "Look at him. I think there really is something wrong."

I can't speak. I gag and cough. It's like when you touch the back of your throat to make yourself sick . . . only it's not me doing the touching. It's the spider! It's trying to get out. I gag again. Something flies out of my mouth and lands on the carpet.

Something wet.

Something furry.

Something disgusting.

We all stare at it. A leg extends from the furry blob — and another and another and another.

That is truly gross, but it's better out than in, I guess.

It starts dragging itself across the carpet toward the door. Toward Craig and Jen.

Jen screams. Craig screams, too. Even louder than Jen.

They both run from the door back to the bed. They are huddled in the corner clutching each other, staring at me in horror.

"Go away!" screams Jen. "Get out!"

So this is what it's like to be the boogeyman. This is what it's like to have people terrified of you. I could get used to this.

I make a big show of licking my lips. I look down at the spider.

"Nice flavor," I say. "But a bit hairy. Either of you want to try it?"

Jen puts a hand over her mouth. Craig goes white.

"What's the matter?" I say. "Aren't you feeling well?"

They shake their heads.

I move toward the door. My work here is done.

"Sweet dreams," I say.

Runaway Baby Carriage

Of all the things I've ever done, this would have to be the most stupid.

I'm lying on my back squashed into a baby carriage. Sucking a pacifier. Waving a Porky Pig rattle. Wearing a diaper.

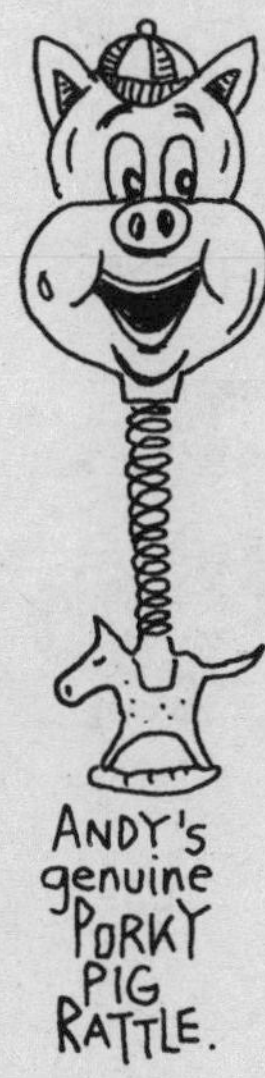
ANDY'S genuine PORKY PIG RATTLE.

Danny is pushing me down the hill. He can hardly walk because he's laughing so hard.

"Goo-goo ga-ga!" I gurgle.

"Good baby," says Danny.

We spent the whole morning walking around the streets inspecting the piles of junk left on everybody's curbs for the garbage collection tomorrow. That's where we found the baby carriage. It's a big old-fashioned one with large wheels, curved fenders, and a high chrome handle. The carriage is a little battered,

but it still goes, and it's got great suspension. And as if that wasn't enough, there was a garbage bag full of old baby clothes and toys to go with it.

Putting on a diaper and going for a ride just seemed like the obvious thing to do.

The pacifier is starting to taste a bit rubbery. I take a deep breath and spit it out. It hits Danny in the eye.

"Bad baby!" says Danny. He lets go of the carriage.

I start to roll down the hill. I scream.

Danny grabs the carriage.

"Just kidding!" he says.

"Good one," I say.

He lets go again.

I roll for a couple more seconds, but this time, I'm only a little bit worried. He grabs the carriage again.

"You're an idiot," I say.

"What am I?" he says.

"An idiot."

He lets go again.

I roll faster this time. He lets me roll about ten feet.

"Danny?" I say.

He laughs and runs to catch me. But just as

JUST PACIFIERS

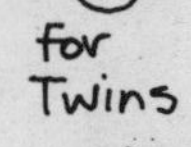

he's about to grab the carriage, he trips and falls flat on his face.

The carriage takes off down the hill. For real this time.

"Danny!" I yell.

I'm flying down the hill. I'd try and jump out, but I'm going too fast. But if I don't jump, I'm going to cross the road at the bottom of the hill and smash into number 21's brick fence.

I see a man watering his lawn. It's Mr. Broadbent, our next-door neighbor.

"Mr. B!" I yell. "Mr. B! Help!"

He turns around.

I'm kneeling in the carriage waving my Porky Pig rattle.

"I can't stop!" I yell. "Stretch your hose across the road!"

He shakes his head and turns back to his watering.

Mr. B and I don't get along too well. I know I can be a little annoying at times, but that's no excuse for ignoring a fellow human being in distress.

"You'll be sorry!" I yell back.

I look over my shoulder at number 21's rapidly approaching brick fence. Actually, I think

it's me who's going to be sorry unless . . . unless . . .

I look at the Porky Pig rattle. I can use it as a brake! I reach down and jam it in the wheel spokes. The rattle shatters. Thanks for nothing, Porky.

What do I do now?

I notice that the carriage is veering slightly to the right. Maybe if I leaned over a little more, I could get around the corner . . . away from the fence and down the next hill.

That hill is even steeper, and it has an intersection at the end. But it does eventually level out, and the traffic shouldn't be too bad at this time of day. It's got to be worth a try.

Mr. Scribble steps on the moon.

I lean over the side and look back at Danny. He's running down the hill, but there's no way he's going to reach me in time.

The carriage is almost tipping over. I'm on two wheels! Sparks are flying off the wheel rims. But it's working. I hear the sound of metal screaming. I close my eyes. I open them again and look over the top of the carriage hood. The hill seems steeper than I remembered — but then I haven't seen it from this perspective before.

I hear barking. I look across the road. It's the pit bull from number 19.

"So long, dog-breath!" I call. He throws himself against the fence.

Everything's going my way now. I've even got a green light at the intersection.

Oh no — I don't believe it!

I *had* a green light.

Now it's yellow.

Now red.

Now I'm in trouble.

The crossroad is full of traffic. On either side, there are cars, buses, trucks, and motorcycles. All ready to take off. Right on top of me.

I have to make them stop. But how?

I know!

I grab the bag of baby gear and pull out a baby doll. It's pretty worn out, but it's still very realistic. It might just do the trick.

"Sorry about this," I say, "but it's either you or me."

I throw the doll as far ahead of the carriage as I can. It lands right in front of all the traffic.

The cars and trucks squeal to a halt. I rocket into the intersection. There's nothing in my way. Well, nothing except for the doll.

The baby carriage hits the doll and flips up into the air. I hang on to the sides as it does a

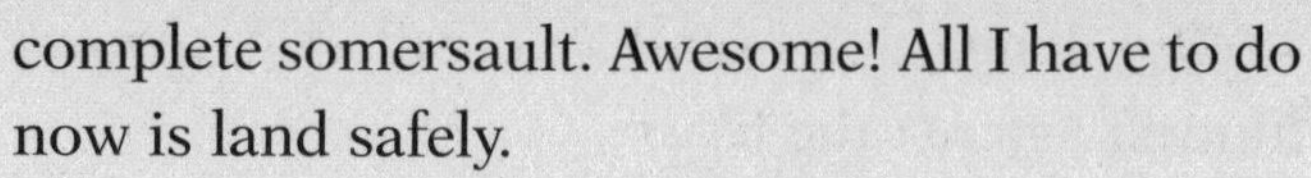

complete somersault. Awesome! All I have to do now is land safely.

I look over the side of the baby carriage. I'm heading for a fire hydrant.

SMASH!

The fire hydrant cap comes off and a fountain of water sprays out the side. It blasts the back of the carriage and sends me hurtling down the stretch of road that I was hoping to slow down on.

I hear a huffing and panting sound behind me. Thank goodness. Danny!

I look around.

Uh-oh.

It's not Danny. It's the pit bull from number 19. He's escaped and is chasing me. He's gaining on me, too.

I grab my bag of baby stuff and pull out the first thing that comes to hand. A plastic bottle. I throw it at the dog. It hits the road and bounces off into the gutter.

I reach into the bag again. I grab something smooth and hard. A container of baby powder. Perfect! I can create a smoke screen that will choke the dog and give me time to disappear.

I throw the powder. It hits the ground. The container explodes. An enormous cloud of perfumed white powder billows out behind me.

But it doesn't stop the dog. He runs straight through it as if it was . . . well . . . baby powder, I guess. The only difference now is that he's whiter. And madder. And he's gaining on me.

I have to speed up! I've got a strong tail-wind. Why not take advantage of it? I remove my diaper. Lucky I kept my undies on. There's a wire coat hanger in the carriage, so I rig the diaper up on a sort of coat hanger sail-frame. The wind catches the diaper and I go speeding forward. Soon the dog is just a speck in the distance.

I hear bells. Uh-oh. Bells can mean only one thing. A railroad crossing!

A train is heading for the crossing and the crossing gate is coming down. But it's okay. I think I'm going fast enough to make it under the gate and across the tracks in time.

I push the carriage hood down so it doesn't catch on the gate and duck down so I don't hit my head.

I come to a sudden stop. I made it under the

crossing gate all right, but now the wheels are stuck in the tracks. The train is almost on top of me.

I close my eyes.

This is it. The big one. What a stupid way to go. Sitting in a baby carriage wearing nothing but a pair of undies.

Then, above the dinging of the bell and the roar of the train, I hear the huffing and panting again.

I look up. It's the dog. Barreling toward me with his head down. He's going to give the carriage the head butt of the century.

"No!" I yell. "Stop! There's no sense in both of us dying!"

WHAM!

The force of the dog hitting the back of the carriage sends me hurtling forward across the tracks, under the crossing gate, and speeding off down the road again.

I look behind me. The train is clattering through the crossing. The dog is nowhere to be seen. But I can't worry about him now — I've got problems of my own.

I'm heading toward two men carrying a large sheet of glass. They see me coming. Their mouths drop open.

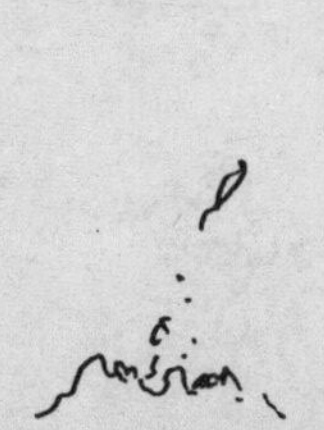

I veer left so that they can keep going across the road. But they go left.

I veer right to try to squeeze through the gap on the other side. But they go right.

"Get out of the way!" I yell.

Now they're just going back and forth, back and forth, back and forth . . .

I notice a road off to the right. I've got to take it. I lean over to get the carriage onto two wheels again.

There is a huge crash of breaking glass. I glance behind me. It's the dog! He's just run right through the sheet of glass. He is indestructible. The men are waving their arms and yelling.

"Stop!" they yell. "Eewayamp!"

What? Are they crazy? Eewayamp? What's an eewayamp?

I turn around. I'm not on a road at all. I'm on a FREEWAY RAMP!

And even worse, I'm heading toward a big red sign that reads WRONG WAY. GO BACK.

I can't. I'm going too fast. I'm going to be on the freeway in seconds.

But the ramp has a sharp bend. There's no way I can make that turn.

I crash into the curb. I fly out of the carriage, over the sign, and over the roadside concrete barrier.

I'm hurtling down into somebody's backyard. This is going to hurt. Think of the biggest and baddest bike accident you've ever had and then multiply it by fifteen thousand. Now take that number and raise it to the power of ten. It's probably going to be about seventeen million times worse than that.

ANDY's Collection of things stuck on rusty nails.

I don't believe it! A trampoline.

I land on my stomach and bounce down so hard that for a moment, I feel the ground through the thin layer of trampoline rubber. But it's only for a moment. I shoot back up into the air. Away from the trampoline. Away from the backyard and toward a high wooden fence. I think I'm going to make it, but it's going to be close.

Piece of Danny's undies.

A piece of Mr. Broadbent's brain.

Mrs. Grove's nose.

I flap my arms to give me extra lift.

I skim over the top of the fence . . . but only just. A nail catches my undies and they're pulled off me as I sail over.

I'm flying through the air.

Naked.

Actually, it's not such a bad feeling. In fact

it's kind of nice. I can feel the wind on places I've never felt the wind on before.

And my luck seems to be holding.

I'm heading for a swimming pool!

It seems strangely familiar.

A man and a woman are lying on lounge chairs by the side of the pool. They seem familiar, too, but I haven't got time to figure out why. I have to prepare for splashdown.

I close my eyes and make my body into an upside-down "V" shape so that I don't go too deep.

SPLASH!

A perfect landing.

I swim to the surface, shake my head, and wipe my eyes.

Uh-oh.

Now I know why the man and the woman look familiar.

It's my dad's boss. And his wife.

"Hi, Mr. Bainbridge! Hi, Mrs. Bainbridge!" I say. "Just thought I'd drop in."

I don't know why they are looking so surprised. It's not like this is the first time I've appeared in front of them, without warning, without my undies. There was the time I got

stuck in their bathroom window. And the time I fell through the dining room roof. But to be fair, I guess this is the most spectacular.

"I guess you're wondering how I got here," I say. "Well, I can explain. . . ."

Mr. Bainbridge holds up his hand.

"No, please don't, Andy," he says, getting up out of his chair. "It's not necessary. I'll just go and call your father."

Mrs. Bainbridge is holding her hands in front of her eyes. Mr. Bainbridge helps her up and they go inside.

I kick back and float across the pool.

I can't believe it. I survived. That was the most terrifying ride of my life.

I can't wait to get home, fix up the baby carriage, and do it all over again.

As far as I'm concerned, the only good thing about fancy restaurants is that they have candles on the tables.

"Watch this," I say to Danny.

I pass my hand slowly through the candle flame and then hold it up to show him the black mark left on my fingers.

"How tough is that?" I say.

"That's nothing," says Danny. "Watch this!"

Danny rolls up his sleeve and passes his hand across the flame. But he doesn't keep going. He stops halfway. The candle is burning him. Danny is crazy.

He jerks his hand out of the flame and shakes it back and forth.

"Ouch, ooch, itch, utch, eech," he says. He bites his lip and looks up at the ceiling.

"I beg your pardon?" I say.

"Hot," he says, shaking his hand. "Really hot!"

Mom gives us a withering look.

"Would you stop that!" she says.

"Stop what?" I say.

"Stop playing with the candles."

"We're not playing," I say. "We're performing amazing feats of bravery and endurance."

She gives me another withering look. It's even more withering than the last one. In fact, it's the witheringest look I've ever received. I'm surprised that the little pink flowers in the middle of the table didn't just keel over and die from it.

"Just don't," she says.

I sigh and slump in my chair.

I thought tonight would be boring — but not this boring. I didn't want to come, but Mom insisted. She won a dinner for four in a radio contest and thought it would be nice to take the family somewhere special. Jen got out of it because it's her boyfriend's birthday. I said I would come only if I could bring Danny along for company.

I don't think Dad is too thrilled to be here, either. He is fidgeting and drumming his fingers on the table.

"Stop that," says Mom. "Do you want everybody to look at us?"

"No," says Dad. "Just the waiter. What do we have to do to get some service around here?"

"Be patient," says Mom. "This is a five-star restaurant, not a fast-food place."

"It is for some people," says Dad, nodding toward a table nearby. "That couple arrived after us and they've already been served drinks, and they've got menus."

I've got something that will get the waiter's attention. Hanging on the back of my chair is my jacket, and in the pocket is a party popper I brought with me.

I reach around to get it, but Danny stops me. He grabs my arm.

"Hey," he whispers. "Isn't that Natasha Teasedale?"

"Where?" I say.

Danny points at the couple Dad was talking about. They are sitting a few tables away from us.

"No," I say. "It can't be."

Firstly, attract the waiter's attention.

Always explore the delights of exotic cuisine.

WHEN YOUR MEAL ARRIVES:

Remember good table manners,

and always spit out the plate.

"It is," says Danny. "Look at her hair. And that's Dirk Gibson with her."

GREAT FEATS AT THE DINNER TABLE #17

The more I look, the more I think Danny might be right. She has curly red hair that cascades down either side of her face and rests in bunches on the tabletop. It's Natasha Teasedale all right. Nobody else in the world has hair like that.

"Wow!" I say.

In case you've just crawled out from under a rock, Natasha Teasedale is the biggest star on television. She's been in millions of shows and movies and won thousands of awards. Her boyfriend, Dirk Gibson, is on television, too, but he's not as big a star as Natasha. He's on the wrestling show where big dumb beefcakes pretend to fight each other. Beats me what she sees in him.

"Should we go and say hello?" says Danny.

"No!" I say.

"Why not?" he says. "Are you chicken?"

"No, I just wouldn't know what to say or do."

"How about, 'Hello'?" says Danny. "And we could give her some flowers."

"Where are we going to get flowers?" I say.

"From there," says Danny, pointing to the

table next to ours. It's all set up with plates and cutlery, and there's a vase of little pink flowers in the middle, but there's nobody sitting at it.

"Okay," I say. "Go on."

"You've got to come, too," says Danny.

"No way," I say. "You saw her first."

"You like her more than me," says Danny.

"Do not."

"Do so."

"But she's with her boyfriend," I say.

"No she's not," says Danny. "Not anymore. He just left the table."

I look over. Danny's right. Natasha is alone. It's now or never.

"Okay," I say. "Let's do it."

We stand up.

"Where are you going?" says Mom.

"We're just going to the toilet," I say.

Mom looks at Dad.

Dad is cleaning his fingernails with his fork. He puts his fork down, looking guilty. "What are you looking at me for?"

"Go with them," says Mom.

"Me?" says Dad. "Why?"

"Well, I can't go," says Mom.

"Actually, we don't need anybody to take us," I say. "We're old enough to go by ourselves."

"Well, don't cause any trouble," says Mom.

"We're only going to the toilet," I say.

"Don't use that tone of voice with me," says Mom. "You know exactly what I mean. Go straight there. Don't play with the toilet handles. Don't lock the stall doors and climb out over the top. Wash your hands when you've finished. Don't have races to see how fast you can empty the soap dispenser. Don't point the hand dryer at your hair and pretend you're rock stars — remember, other people have to use the restrooms as well as you."

I give Mom a withering look.

"How old do you think I am?"

"Do I have to answer that?"

"Come on, Danny," I say.

"And don't throw your pants out the window!" calls Mom.

We walk quickly away from the table before Mom can say anything else embarrassing. I don't want Natasha to hear.

"Grab the flowers," whispers Danny.

I take the flowers from the vase.

Danny and I are both very nervous.

We walk up to Natasha's table. Up close, she is even more beautiful than she is on television.

"Hello," I say.

Natasha is concentrating on her menu. She doesn't hear me.

I clear my throat and try again.

"Um, excuse me," I say. "Natasha?"

She looks up.

"No autographs, boys," she says with a sigh. "I'm relaxing, okay?"

"We don't want autographs," I say. I offer her the flowers, which are dripping. "We just wanted to give you these."

Her face softens.

"Why, thank you," she says.

"They're from me, too," says Danny. He reaches across the table to try to give them to her as well. He can be so childish sometimes.

As he reaches, he bumps my arm and I knock over a candle. It falls out of the holder and rolls across the table toward Natasha. The flame connects with her frizzy curls and climbs up her hair in an instant.

This is unbelievable. We just wanted to say hello — not set her hair on fire.

There is an almost-full glass of soda on the table. I pick it up and throw it at her burning

hair. It puts the fire out. Apart from being wet, her hair hardly looks any different. If it wasn't for the smell, you wouldn't even know there'd been a fire. I'm a hero.

"How dare you!" she splutters. "How dare you throw soda in my face!"

I must have been too quick. Natasha doesn't seem to realize what has happened. Before I can explain, she picks up her glass of root beer and throws it at me.

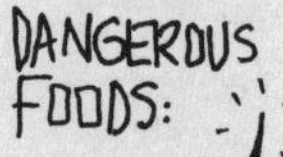

I duck.

She looks past me and puts her hand over her mouth. I turn around.

Sharpened banana.

It's Dirk. The root beer has gone all over his shirt. He looks like he's splattered with mud.

"Sorry, Dirk," she says. "I wasn't aiming for you. It was meant for him."

"Why?" says Dirk. "Did he hurt you?"

"He threw soda in my face," says Natasha.

"He what?" says Dirk. His face goes as red as his shirt.

A lit apple.

He picks up a breadstick. It's a giant one — more like a club than a breadstick.

"I'll teach you to throw soda in a lady's face," he says.

"No, you don't understand," I say. "Her hair was on fire."

Greek Snail

"You set her hair on fire?" he says.

"Yes," I say. "Well, no. I mean I did, but I didn't mean to. I was just giving her some flowers."

"They were from me as well," says Danny.

Dirk's face is twisted with rage.

"You tried to give my girlfriend flowers?"

I'm backed up against the table next to Natasha's. Dirk steps toward me. I realize that nothing I can say will calm him down.

I reach behind me for a weapon. My hands close on something soft and oily. I look down. I've got three olives.

"Stop right there!" I say to Dirk.

But he keeps right on coming.

I throw one of the olives at him. He uses the breadstick to bat it clear across the restaurant. It hits the front window and splatters like a bug on a windshield.

"Andy!" yells Mom. "Stop that!"

She is standing up, hands on her hips, glaring at me.

"What about him?" I say.

Mom looks at Dirk.

"You stop it, too," she says.

But Dirk doesn't stop. He takes a step toward me.

I throw another olive. Dirk bats it into the chandelier and sets it spinning. It creates a sort of disco-ball effect, throwing little circles of light around the room.

"Stop it, Dirk!" screams Natasha.

"Just let me hit him once," he says. He raises the breadstick over his shoulder.

I throw my last olive. Dirk bats it straight back at me. It's like a bullet. It hits me in the chest with such force that I am propelled backward onto a tabletop.

I look up. I see the surprised faces of two old ladies above me.

"Excuse me," I say. "A little accident . . ."

"Accident nothing," says one of the ladies. "It was that brute's fault."

"I've never liked Dirk Gibson," says the other lady, putting a little bowl of pepper into my hand. "He's nothing but a big bully. Give him this from us."

"Thanks," I say. It's just what I need. And just in time.

Dirk picks me up by my collar. He's frothing at the mouth. I throw the pepper into his face. The reaction is instant.

"Ah-ah-ah . . . CHOO!"

Right in my face. I'm blown back across

the table. Dirk staggers around blindly and crashes into the waiter who is carrying a tray of drinks.

The waiter stumbles backward into my dad's lap. Dirk lands on top of them both. Dad's chair collapses and they end up in a sprawling heap on top of him.

"Get off me, you big ape!" yells Dad.

"I beg your pardon, sir," says the waiter.

"I wasn't talking to you," says Dad. "I was talking to that gorilla on top of us."

"Are you calling me a gorilla?" says Dirk, getting to his feet.

Dad wriggles out from underneath the waiter and stands up. "On second thought, no," says Dad, brushing himself off. "Because it's an insult to gorillas. I'd say somebody who picks on people smaller than himself is more accurately described as a coward."

WHO'S INSULTING GORILLAS?

"Go, Mr. G!" calls Danny.

"Shut up, Danny!" says Dad.

"You just made a big mistake, fella," says Dirk. "Nobody calls Dirk Gibson a coward and gets away with it."

"Oh knock it off, Dirk," says Natasha.

But Dirk's not listening. He is bearing down on Dad. Dad is backing away. He looks behind

him at a large display of fruit. He picks up a pineapple.

USING A PINEAPPLE IN COMBAT.

"Don't come any closer," says Dad. "I've got a pineapple . . . and I'm not afraid to use it."

Dirk laughs.

"Just try it!" he says.

Grasp in left hand.

"If you insist," says Dad.

Dad whacks Dirk over the head with the pineapple. Dirk staggers around looking dazed. His legs buckle underneath him and he slumps to the ground. You can almost see the birds and stars circling above him.

"Good one, Mr. G!" says Danny.

Mom appears beside us. She has my jacket in her hand.

"Come on," she says. "We're leaving before you can do any more damage."

RUN!!

"But what about our food?" says Danny.

"Never mind your food," says the waiter. He's kneeling on the floor, putting the broken glasses back on the tray. "I think it's best for everyone if you leave now. There is a fast-food place at the end of the street. You might feel more at home there."

Mom gives him one of her withering looks.

He gives her one back.

She huffs, turns, and walks straight into an ice bucket on a stand. It clatters to the floor and she falls on top of it. Dad rushes to help her.

"Oh no," says Danny, grabbing my arm. "Look!"

I turn around.

The noise seems to have woken Dirk out of his stupor. He shakes his head and looks at us.

"Quick," says Danny. "Run!"

"Oh no you don't!" roars Dirk.

We are heading for the door. Danny is just ahead of me. We are almost at the dessert display case near the front register. I look back. Too late.

Dirk leaps and tackles me to the ground. I'm scrambling to get away, but he's holding me tightly around my waist, boa constrictor style. He's going to squeeze me to death.

"Help me, Danny!" I gasp.

Danny runs around to the back of the dessert case and grabs a strawberry shortcake.

"Let go of him!" says Danny, balancing the strawberry shortcake on one hand.

"Not until he's learned his lesson," says Dirk, squeezing me even tighter.

When your enemy is about to CRUSH YOU TO DEATH, YOU CAN
(a) CALL FOR YOUR MOM!!
(b) Explain to him that you are suffering from the DEADLY EBOLA VIRUS.
(c) CALL For the

"Have it your way," says Danny. "I just hope you're hungry."

He pushes the strawberry shortcake into Dirk's face. Dirk yells and lets go of me to wipe the whipped cream and strawberries from his eyes. I quickly wriggle away.

Dirk gets up and lunges at Danny.

Danny jumps up onto the dessert display case, leaps for the chandelier, and swings himself clear across the restaurant.

Dirk turns back to me.

I run to the corner, pull a table over, and barricade myself against the wall.

Dirk reaches over the top of the table.

I see a fork on the floor. I pick it up and stab at his hand.

He shrieks and pulls his arm away.

He tries to grab the table and pull it away from the wall. I stab him again.

"For heaven's sake, control your boys," the waiter yells at Mom and Dad. "They are destroying the restaurant."

Dad points at Dirk. "What about him?" he says. "He started it!"

"Yeah," says the lady who passed me the pepper, "the big ugly brute!"

"He is not ugly," says Natasha.

"You would say that, you floozy!" says the lady. She grabs a bowl of fruit salad and tips it over Natasha's head.

Danny rushes to Natasha's aid.

"Leave her alone!" he says, grabbing the pepper-lady's hair.

"No, Danny!" I yell. "She's on our side!"

But it's too late. Danny pushes the pepper-lady's face into a bowl of soup. Her friend throws an omelette at Danny. He ducks, and it wraps around the head of a man at the next table. The man's wife retaliates by throwing a huge plate of seafood at Danny.

Her throw is wild, and the stuff on the plate goes everywhere. Pieces of fish, shrimp, crabs, squid, oysters, and lots of other squishy things are flung across the room. Almost everyone in the restaurant is hit by something.

Suddenly, everybody seems to be involved. Food is flying in all directions — appetizers, main courses, desserts — you name it, people are throwing it. Even Mom is hurling stuff. She's not exactly hitting anyone, but she seems to be enjoying herself all the same.

Dirk smashes a chair against my table. "Are you a man or a mouse?" he roars. "Come out and fight!"

"Dirk! That's enough!" screams Natasha above the noise.

But nothing will stop Dirk. He is on a mission. A mission to destroy me.

If only I had my party popper.

I look around for my jacket. It's lying on the floor where Mom dropped it when she fell over the ice bucket.

I come out from behind the barricade. Dirk is in such a frenzy that he doesn't see me. I grab a tablecloth and put it over my head.

I crawl toward my jacket.

Somebody is hitting me with something hard.

I peer out from under the tablecloth. It's Danny. He's whacking me with a lobster.

"Knock it off, you moron," I say. "It's me."

"Sorry," says Danny.

I make it to my jacket and fumble in the pocket for the popper. Got it!

I stand up. Something wet and spongy hits me in the face. I fall down and drop the popper.

I look up.

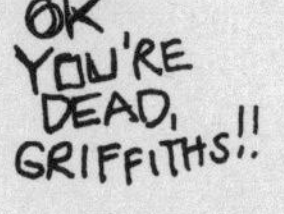

Oh no. Dirk has seen me. He's seen the popper, too.

He dives to the floor. We are both scram-

bling for the popper. He grabs it and holds it inches away from my face.

"Got you now, you little weasel," he says.

"Watch out," says Dad. "He's got a party popper!"

"I know that, Dad," I say, not taking my eyes off the popper for a second.

"Don't worry," says Danny. "I've got you covered."

We both look up. Danny is standing on top of the bar. He's holding a bottle of champagne, his thumbs poised on the cork. "Drop it, Dirk!"

Dirk stares at him.

"You keep out of this," he says. "This is none of your business."

"His business is my business," says Danny. He shakes the bottle and takes aim. "Drop it or I'll blow you into the middle of next week."

Dirk hesitates for a moment and then drops the popper.

"Stupid kids," he says.

He stands up and turns to Natasha.

"Come on," he says, "let's get out of here."

"No way," she says. "I'm not going anywhere with you."

"But . . ."

"It's over, Dirk."

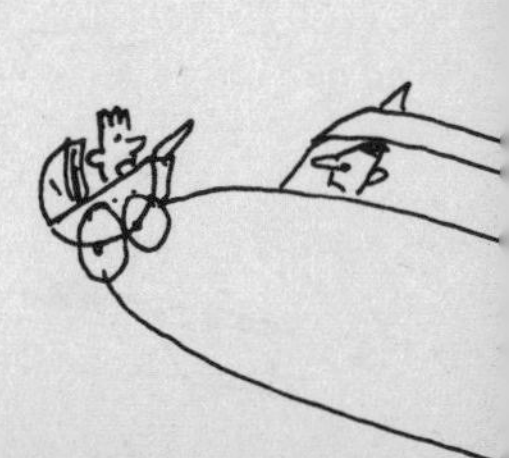

She takes off an enormous engagement ring and throws it at him.

"I was only trying to protect you," he says.

"That's what you always say," she says. "And you always end up making it worse."

People start applauding. Natasha looks radiant. It's one of the greatest performances of her career — and we're seeing it live.

Dirk bends down and picks up the ring.

"You're all crazy!" he yells, and barges out of the restaurant.

Everybody in the restaurant applauds.

I stand up.

Danny jumps down off the bar and we high-five each other.

Natasha comes over to us.

"I just wanted to thank you both," she says.

"Don't mention it," I say.

"No, really," she says. "I've never seen anybody stand up to Dirk the way you did today. And to think I was going to marry that brute. You've shown me just how violent and bad-tempered he really is. You were very brave, and I'd like to give you a reward."

"No, please," I say. "It's not necessary. . . ."

"Close your eyes," says Natasha. "Both of you."

I can't believe it! She's going to kiss me! This

is turning out to be the best night of my life. A food fight in a fancy restaurant *and* a kiss from Natasha Teasedale.

Dad steps between Danny and me. "I helped, too," he says. He closes his eyes and puts his head forward. Mom pulls him back by the arm.

"No you don't," she says, giving him one of her withering looks.

Natasha giggles. "What are you waiting for?" she says to me. "Don't you want your reward?"

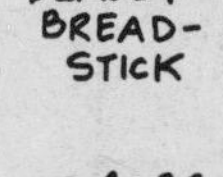

I close my eyes. Life doesn't get any better than this.

WHACK!

I feel a sharp pain on the top of my head. I open my eyes.

She's holding a breadstick in her hand.

"That's for setting my hair on fire," she says.

"But . . ."

She raises the breadstick and brings it down again.

WHACK!

"And that's for throwing soda in my face!"

Danny is bent over laughing.

"Something funny?" she says.

"Yes," says Danny. "You are. That was amazing. He had it coming."

"You want to see it again?" she says, raising

the breadstick above her head in a two-handed grip.

* that's WHACK spelled backwards.

"Yes, please!" says Danny.

WHACK!

She brings the breadstick down again, but this time not on my head—on Danny's. He's not laughing anymore. Just standing there with the bottle of champagne in his hand, looking dazed. Natasha drops the breadstick and heads for the door. The waiter runs after her.

"Mademoiselle Teasedale," he says. "I am so sorry!"

She stops and turns around.

"It's okay," she says.

"No, it is not okay," he says. "It is not okay at all."

"No, you're right," she says. "It isn't." She walks back to her breadstick, picks it up, and hits the waiter over the head.

Boy, that's some temper she's got. But it's understandable, what with the pressure of being so famous and having to learn all those lines and act and sign autographs and everything.

She's about to go through the door. Suddenly there is a loud pop. It's Danny's champagne bottle.

Domestic snail.

"Oops," says Danny.

The cork fires out and hits Natasha fair and square on the side of the head. It ricochets and shoots straight up into the chandelier. The chandelier blows apart and beads of polished glass rain down over the restaurant. It is a beautiful end to a brilliant performance.

Natasha stops, straightens her shoulders, turns around, and gives us a look even more withering than one of Mom's withering looks. Then she turns and walks out of the restaurant without saying a word.

Wow.

What a professional.

What dignity.

What poise.

You've got to hand it to her. She's had her hair set on fire, soda thrown in her face, fruit salad tipped all over her, broken up with her boyfriend, and just taken a direct hit in the side of the head from a champagne cork, and yet she can still walk out of the restaurant with style.

She's a great actress. There's no doubt about it. And if I ever see her again, I'm going to tell her that.

Snail Aid

I'm standing at the entrance to the park, trying to decide whether to go in. I know it's dangerous, but I want to get home before the rain starts again, and I'll get there a lot quicker if I cut through the park. I hear thunder. I decide to risk it.

I walk through the gate.

I'm not sure if this was such a good idea after all. There are snails all over the gravel path. I have to walk very slowly to avoid stepping on them. If there's one sound I hate, it's the sound of a snail shell being crushed. I think I hate the sound even more than the snail does.

But so far so good.

I've almost made it to the pond in the mid-

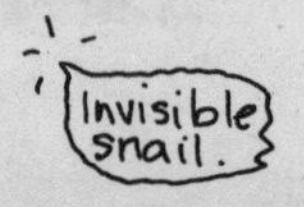

dle of the park. No crushed snails and, even better, no sign of my enemy. I look up at the old birch tree just to make sure.

But it's there.

The mad crow.

Waiting.

For me.

I look around to make sure there is nobody else in the park. The place is deserted. That's good.

I open my bag, take out an ice-cream container, and put it on my head. I know it's not a good look, but it's better than having a hole pecked in the top of my skull. That's not a particularly good look, either.

I take a deep breath and start running.

There is an explosion of swooping, flapping, and clicking around my ears.

Even though I've got my container helmet on, I'm still scared. What if the crow goes for my eyes? What if it pecks them out and feeds them to its babies? I'll be able to see myself being eaten!

The crow seems to be everywhere at once.

There is an especially hard whack on the side of the container.

I stagger sideways.

CRUNCH!

I look down at a gray-and-brown pasty mess.

A snail! I stepped on a snail!

I look up at the crow. It's getting ready to swoop at me again.

"All right," I yell, "you asked for it!"

I reach into my bag and pull out my gun.

The crow is swooping down fast.

I point the gun at it. My hand is shaking. I steady it with my other hand and squeeze the trigger.

POW! POW! POW!

The crow veers steeply into the air and flies back toward its tree. It's only a cap gun, but the crow doesn't know that. I blow the end of the gun and slide it into my pocket.

I kneel down and look at the snail. It is blowing bubbles. It's alive.

I've crushed its shell, but not completely. The basic shape is still there. Maybe . . . just maybe . . . I could put it back together again. Like a jigsaw puzzle. It's worth a try.

"I'm really sorry," I say. "But don't worry — I think I can rebuild you."

The snail blows a little green bubble. That's

a good sign. Well, I think it is — sometimes it's hard to tell with snails.

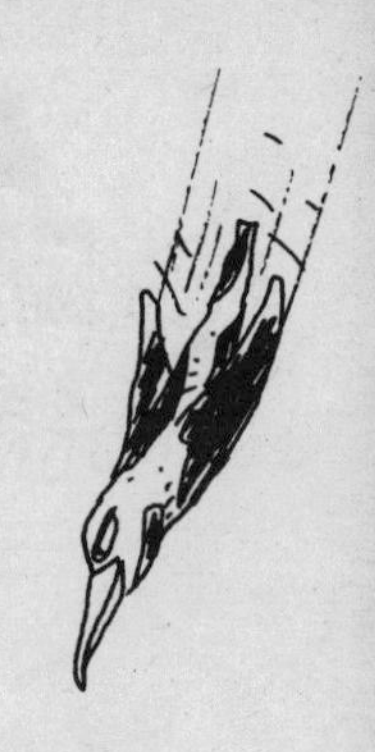

There's a picnic table near the pond. I can use it for the operation. I take my library card out of my pocket. I slide it slowly underneath the snail and lift it up.

The crow is nowhere to be seen, but I put my hand over the top of the snail to protect it, just in case the crow tries to launch a surprise attack. I run, crouching at the same time. This is a war zone.

We make it safely to the table. The top of the table is wet and dirty. I fish around in my pocket and find a handkerchief. It's got a huge blob of old chewing gum stuck to it. I was saving it for an emergency — and here it is.

I lay the handkerchief out flat on the table. I bet real surgeons don't have to work under these conditions.

I ease the snail off my library card and onto the handkerchief.

Luckily I've got a glue stick in my bag. I get it out, but it's hard to know exactly how to start. The glue stick is jumbo-size and the pieces of snail shell are so tiny. And the edges are so thin.

I look over at the birch tree to check on the crow. I can't see it, but I notice that the birch tree has long white pieces of papery bark curling off it. It gives me an idea. I could smear glue onto the bark, wrap it around the snail, and use the strands of chewing gum to hold it all together while the glue dries. Just like a plaster cast.

"Stay there," I say to the snail. "I'll be right back."

I sprint across to the tree.

The bark is wet. I rip a few sheets off to get to the dry stuff underneath.

"Hey you!" says a voice behind me. "Can't you read the sign?"

I turn around.

A man in green overalls is sitting in what looks like a little golf cart. He must be the park ranger.

"What sign?" I say, backing away from the tree and up onto the grass.

"That sign," he says, pointing at the base of the tree.

I look at the little sign. It says KEEP OFF THE GRASS.

"Sorry," I say. "I just needed some bark."

"So does the tree," says the ranger. "In

fact, the tree needs it a whole lot more than you do."

"No, you don't understand," I say. "It's not for me, it's for a snail. . . ."

But the ranger is not interested in my explanation. He's already tearing off across the grass in search of more criminals.

It doesn't matter, anyway. I've got the bark. I head back toward the table.

I realize I'm still wearing the container on my head. How embarrassing!

I go to take it off, but suddenly the air is filled with the sound of flapping and clicking. It's the crow! Back already. I start ducking and weaving, but it doesn't try to attack me.

I look up. The crow is heading back to its nest. What was that all about?

I reach the table.

I don't believe it.

The snail is gone!

I know what that crow was up to. It was on a snail-stealing raid. My poor snail is about to become baby crow food.

But not if I can help it.

I run to the tree and start climbing.

The crow goes beserk. I bet nobody has ever dared come this close to its nest before.

The bird does a midair U-turn and zeros in on me.

I see a small blob falling through the air. My snail!

It splashes into the pond.

This is terrible. The pond is full of goldfish! My snail is in even more danger than before.

I pull my cap gun out of my pocket and fire it at the crow. The crow flees skyward.

I run to the edge of the pond. There's something going on in the middle. The fish are all in one spot. They're probably fighting over who's going to eat my snail.

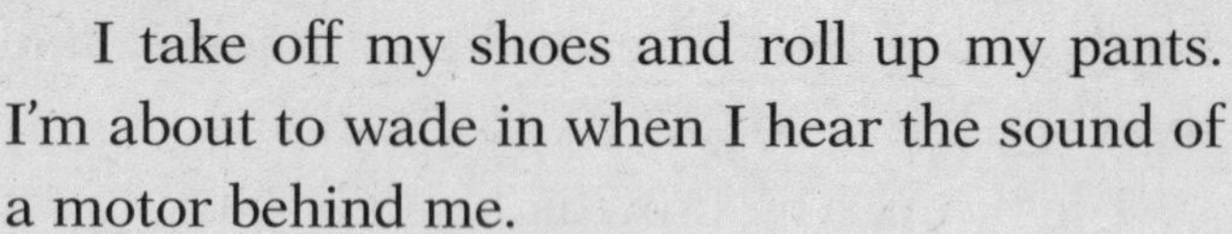

I take off my shoes and roll up my pants. I'm about to wade in when I hear the sound of a motor behind me.

"Hey you!" says the park ranger through a megaphone. "Can't you read the sign?"

"What sign?" I say.

He points to the sign on the side of the pond. It says NO SWIMMING.

"But my snail!" I say. "I have to save my snail!"

"I don't care if you have to save your mother!" he says. "The sign says no swimming!"

He tears off again before I can argue. I'm

Answer to Pg 3 QUIZ:
The next word in the series is:
(Do you speak ancient Egyptian?)

getting really sick of this man and his stupid signs. He just doesn't get it. This is not about saving my mother. This is an emergency. This is about saving my snail. If it's not already too late, that is.

I kneel down and lean forward to look into the pond. The ice-cream container falls off my head and splashes into the water. The fish scatter. I have a brilliant idea. I can use the container to scoop up the fish. I look around to check there's no signs that say NO SCOOPING. No — only one that says NO FISHING. But I'm not going to fish — I'm going to scoop. I grab the container and use it to try to catch the fish, but I can't reach them. The pond's too deep.

Then I have another brilliant idea. I go over to the NO FISHING sign. It is nailed to a wooden stake. I pull the stake out of the ground and remove the sign. I take out the nail and use it to attach my container to the stake. I now have a scoop that can reach right into the middle of the pond. And best of all, I won't be breaking any rules. As far as I can see, there is no sign around here saying DO NOT DISMANTLE THE NO FISHING SIGN AND TURN IT INTO A SCOOP.

Andy's fish scoop.

I scoop my container into the pond and catch two of the biggest and fattest goldfish I can find. One of the fish has big, ugly bugged-out eyes. I pick it up. I peer into the fish's gaping mouth. My snail is stuck in its throat. No wonder the fish's eyes are bugging out.

Now I've got the snail — all I have to do is get it out of the fish. But how? Tickle it? Tell it a joke and make it laugh? What sort of jokes do fish find funny? I'm trying to think of a fish joke when the fish wriggles out of my hand and falls to the ground. It flip-flops around on the grass and the snail pops out of its mouth.

Why did the fish cross the road?

I throw the fish back into the pond and rush my snail to the operating table.

Amazingly, most of the snail's shell is still there. But there's no time to lose.

I paste little pieces of paperbark over the broken pieces of shell to help hold it all together. I tear some small bits of green plastic off the cover of my school notebook and use them to replace the missing pieces of shell.

I stand back and admire my work. Looks cool. A brown-and-green snail. And not only does it look good, it's great camouflage as well. The other snails are going to be so jealous.

My snail seems pretty happy with its new shell, too. It's frothing and bubbling with excitement. Well, frothing and bubbling, anyway. Like I said, it's hard to tell with snails.

I wrap long strands of chewing gum around the snail's shell to hold it all together while the glue dries.

Done. Good as new. Better than new. And stronger. I think I could whack this snail with a hammer and the hammer would just bounce off. Not that I'm actually going to try it. I've put this snail through enough trauma for one day.

I put the snail down in the grass and kneel beside it.

"Go now, little snail," I whisper. I want to say more. I want to tell it how sorry I am and that I will never step on another snail for as long as I live. I want to tell it that I will dedicate my life to fighting for the rights of snails so that they can travel the sidewalks of the world free from the fear of being stepped on. But I can't say any of this. I'm too choked up.

As I watch it begin its slide to freedom, I feel a mixture of awe and pride. I'm like those people who save beached whales. Only I've done more than just save the snail, I've improved it.

I'm still waving good-bye to the snail half an hour later when I hear the golf cart again.

I look up.

Uh-oh. The park ranger is over at the pond, looking at my ice-cream container scoop. I left it beside the pond. And the other fish is still in it. Oops!

"What's this fish doing in here?" he says.

"Um . . . would you believe it jumped?" I say. "I wouldn't be surprised if you didn't believe me because it *was* pretty incredible. I've never seen anything like it before. It just leaped out of the water and landed in the container."

From the look on his face, it is obvious he doesn't believe me.

He picks up my scoop.

"Can't you read the sign?" he barks. He points to where the NO FISHING sign was. He looks. No sign. He looks at the wooden stake in his hand. He looks at the NO FISHING sign lying on the grass.

He turns back to me. His eyes are bulging. He looks a little like one of the fish. He pours the water and the fish back into the pond and wrenches the container off the wooden stake.

CHAOS THEORY
cont' from Pg 73.

"All right, you troublemaker," he says. "I've had enough. I want you out of my park!"

"But you don't understand," I say.

"No, *you* don't understand!" he says. "This park is my responsibility. All the plants and animals here are in my care and you are threatening their well-being!"

"But I saved a snail," I say.

He is not listening. He is walking toward me slowly, still holding the wooden stake. He slaps it into the palm of his hand.

"Are you going to leave or do I have to make you?" he says.

"Now don't do anything you might regret," I say, backing away slowly.

"Oh, I won't regret it," he says, slapping his hand with the stake again.

I reach for my cap gun.

"Don't come any closer," I say, pointing it at him.

He laughs and keeps right on coming.

I squeeze the trigger. Nothing.

I squeeze it again. Still nothing.

Drat! Out of caps.

I'm about to step back when something stops me. I look behind me.

My snail.

If I step back, I'll squash it. Again. But if I don't take the step, the ranger will get me for sure.

It's me or the snail. I have to take that step. But I can't. I can't do it. I made a promise.

The ranger grabs my collar.

"Gotcha!" he says.

I suppose there are worse ways to die than being strangled by an insane park ranger. I'm not sure what they are right at the moment, but I'm sure they exist.

Suddenly, there is a flurry of black. Clicking and flapping. The crow! I knew there was a worse way to die.

I can't run because the ranger is holding my collar so tight. I close my eyes and get ready to accept my fate. Any moment, that enormous black beak will penetrate my skull and it will all be over. I hope I go to heaven and get a pair of angel wings. First thing I'll do is come back to the park and dive-bomb the crow. See how much it likes it.

What's taking so long?

I open my eyes. Just in time to see the crow score a direct hit. But not on me. On the park ranger.

He screams. He lets go of my collar and starts running. The crow flies up into the air, circles, and prepares to swoop at him again.

It is a beautiful sight. Almost as beautiful as the sight of my snail still sliding slowly across the grass to freedom. But not quite. Nothing can compare to that.

Who Am I?

Voices.

I hear voices.

I open my eyes.

Everything's blurred.

I close my eyes and open them again.

Round shapes against a white sky. But still blurred. And my head hurts.

I feel a hand shaking my shoulder. The two round shapes merge into one and a face appears. It comes in close. I try to make out who it is, but the face does not look familiar to me.

"Andy!" says the face. "Are you okay?"

"Who's Andy?" I say.

"You're Andy," says the face.

"Who are you?" I say.

"You know me!" says the face. "I'm Danny. Your best friend. You just got hit in the head. Don't you remember? We were trying to make a jack-in-the-box. You were just about to test it, but it went off in your face. I can't believe you don't remember it."

Danny? Jack-in-the-box? My head hurts, that's for sure, but I don't remember getting hit. I don't remember anything about a jack-in-the-box. And I don't remember anyone called Danny.

"I don't know what you're talking about," I say.

"Try sitting up," he says.

"I think I'm going to be sick," I say.

"I'd better get you inside," he says.

He helps me to my feet. The ground is spongy. It's like walking on a mattress.

I look around me. We're in somebody's backyard. There is a clothesline in the center. It's bent over at a forty-five–degree angle, one of the corners practically sticking into the ground. There's a half burned-down fence running alongside the driveway. In the garage there's a mangled baby carriage that looks like it's been run over by a truck. The whole area

looks like it should be cordoned off with yellow tape and declared a disaster area.

JUST MOTHERS:
She's the one who:

eats your brussels sprouts for you.

"Where am I?" I say.

"In your backyard," says the boy.

"My backyard?" I say.

He sighs.

"Take it easy up the steps," he says.

I wobble my way to the top of the porch.

The boy opens a sliding glass door and guides me through it. Inside the house, it's dark and cool.

"Mrs. G!" he calls. "Mrs. G! Come quick! Andy's been hurt!"

"Who's Mrs. G?" I say.

"That's your mother," he says. "You must remember your own mother."

"No," I say. "I can't remember anything."

The boy looks around the room. He grabs my arm and leads me over to a shelf full of photographs.

He points to one of a man and a woman.

"That's your mom," he says, pointing to the woman.

"And who's the guy with the big ears?" I say.

"That's your dad," he says. "But you'd better not let him hear you saying he's got big ears. He goes ballistic."

Hmmm. He's obviously got a bad temper. That would explain the state of the backyard.

"Here's a photo of you," he says.

He's pointing to a picture of a group of people in a restaurant. They are all staring at someone in a gorilla suit. The gorilla has spaghetti all over its head.

I recognize the man and woman from the other photo, but nobody else looks familiar.

"Which one am I?" I say.

"You're the one in the gorilla suit," he says. "Remember? You gave Jen a gorillagram for her birthday and she spilled spaghetti all over you."

"Jen?" I say. "Who's Jen?"

"Your sister," he says, pointing to the girl in the middle of the photo.

"She looks nice," I say.

The boy looks at me closely.

"You really do have amnesia, don't you?" he says.

"I don't know," I say. "I can't remember."

"Mrs. G?" he calls again.

Nobody answers.

"The mother must be out," I say.

"Not *the* mother," he says. "*Your* mother.

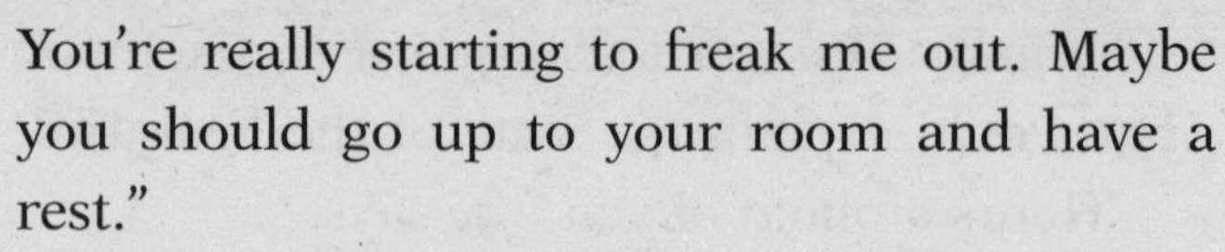

You're really starting to freak me out. Maybe you should go up to your room and have a rest."

"Yeah," I say. "Maybe you're right."

"Somebody will be home soon," he says. "I'll drop by later and see how you are."

"Okay," I say. "But where's the bedroom?"

"Upstairs. The one with the big red skull on the door," he says. "You can't miss it."

"Thanks," I say. "I'm glad I met you."

"Get some rest," he says. "I'll see you later."

I go up the stairs and find the door with the skull on it. Underneath the skull, there's a sign that says ANDY'S ROOM. DANGER! ENTER AT YOUR OWN RISK!

I walk in.

Wow, what an amazing smell. Sort of like a locker room crossed with a garbage can. And the mess! It looks like a bomb went off. Not a normal bomb, though. One filled with undies, socks, and towels. They're everywhere. Hanging off the light, the curtain rods, and the desk.

There is a gorilla suit thrown across the bed. A half-eaten banana on the floor. A fish tank full of green slimy water on the windowsill.

And the bookshelves have some very weird

stuff on them. A severed hand. A jar with an eyeball in it. And a horrible pink teddy bear with a human skull for a head.

What sort of boy is this Andy?

I look at a photograph on a corkboard. The boy has his thumbs jammed in the corners of his mouth and his pointer fingers in the corners of his eyes. He is pulling his eyes down and his mouth up. And sticking his tongue out as well. What an idiot.

I look in a mirror. I don't look anything like that. I can't be this boy. Whoever I am, I'm not Andy. Unless . . . I'd better just do a quick check. I rest the photo against the mirror. I put my thumbs in my mouth and my fingers in my eyes and try to pinch my fingers and thumbs together. I stick my tongue out.

The resemblance is uncanny.

But this can't be right! I can't be Andy. He's sick! He's disturbed! Me looking like him is just a coincidence. Yeah, that's it. Just some sort of crazy coincidence. I don't belong here. Somewhere, somebody's probably missing me. I bet they're really worried. I know! I'll call the police and see if anybody has reported me missing.

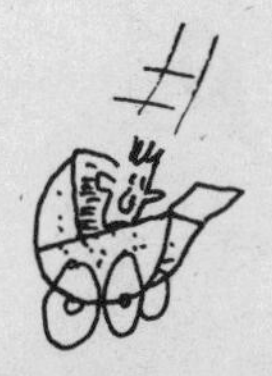

I go downstairs and find a telephone. I call the police.

"Hello," I say. "I'd like to see if anybody has reported me missing."

"I see. . . ." says the man on the other end of the phone. "What is your name?"

"I can't remember," I say.

"You can't remember?"

"No," I say. "That's why I'm calling you. I think I might be missing, and I wanted to see if anybody is looking for me."

"Is this a prank call?" says the man.

"No," I say. "It's not a prank call. I'm serious."

"So let me get this straight," he says. "You're the missing person?"

"Yes," I say. "I think so."

"Can you describe your exact location at this moment?" he says.

"Yes," I say. "I'm in a house talking on the telephone."

"Excellent," says the man. "Case solved."

"Huh?" I say.

"Well," says the man, "as far as I can figure it, if you are the missing person in question, then you just found yourself, so you're no longer missing. Good-bye."

He hangs up. That wasn't really as helpful

as I'd hoped. Just my luck to get the new guy. And my head is starting to hurt again.

I sit down on the couch.

There is a pile of books on the coffee table. I pick one up. *Coping with a Problem Child*. I pick up another one. *Your Nongifted Child*. Under that is one called *Smack Your Child to Success*.

Gee, that Jen must be a real troublemaker.

The glass door slides open. I look up. It's the woman from the photo, the man with the big ears, and the girl called Jen. They are carrying plastic bags.

"Well," says Big Ears, "don't just sit there — give us some help."

"Excuse me," I say, "who am I?"

"Andy, this is no time for a game of twenty questions," he says. "Get up off that couch and help us with these bags."

"So, I'm Andy, am I?" I say.

"Andy," says Big Ears, "if you don't get those bags into the kitchen in the next ten seconds, I swear I will . . ."

"Okay, okay," I say.

I was right. He has got a bad temper. Best not to get him too upset. I pick up the bags and put them on the kitchen table.

"Well, what are you waiting for?" says the mother, sighing. "This stuff isn't going to put itself away."

I put my hand into a bag. I pull out a box of laundry detergent.

"Where does this go?" I say.

"In the cupboard in the laundry room," says the mother. "Where do you think?"

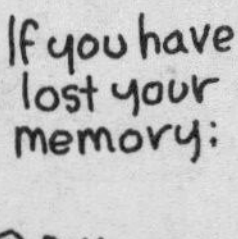

"Where's the laundry room?" I say.

The mother takes the box out of my hands.

"On second thought, don't worry about it," she says. "It will be quicker to do it myself."

"Mrs. G," I say, "you think I'm your son, don't you?"

"Yes," she says. "What bad luck!"

Big Ears snorts. "That's what they told us at the hospital," he says, "but I think there must have been a mix-up."

"Really?" I say. This could explain everything. "Do you think there's any way of checking?"

"Try the zoo," says the girl. "They're probably looking for you right now."

"The zoo?" I say. I guess it's worth a try.

I turn to the mother.

"Would you be able to take me there?" I say.

"Where?" she says.

"To the zoo," I say.

"No!" she says. "What is the matter with you, Andy? Why all these stupid questions?"

"I've lost my memory!" I say. "I don't know who I am. I don't know who you are."

"Very funny," says the mother.

"It's true!" I say. "I don't think I'm who you think I am."

"This is a bad time for another one of your incomprehensible jokes, young man," says Big Ears. "You're already skating on thin ice bringing home a report card with five E's."

"Five E's?" I say. "What's wrong with five E's? Doesn't E stand for excellent?"

The girl snorts.

"Five E's for EEEEEDIOT!" she says.

The mother sighs again.

"What about that talk we had last night?" she says. "Don't you remember what you promised?"

"No," I say. "That's what I'm trying to tell you. I don't remember anything."

Big Ears screws up his face.

"So let me get this straight," he says. "You don't remember anything?"

"No," I say.

"You don't remember who you are?"

"No."

"You don't remember your name?"

"I think it's Andy," I say, "but only because that's what everybody keeps calling me."

"I see," says Big Ears. "Well the best cure for amnesia is to do the things you normally do in a familiar environment. That should help jog your memory."

"But what sort of things do I normally do?" I say. "I can't remember. What am I like?"

"Well for a start, you're really annoying," says the girl. "You play really dumb tricks and you do really stupid things."

"Really?" I say.

The mother laughs.

"No, no, no," she says. "That's just Jen having a little joke."

I was right. That girl is a troublemaker.

The girl looks annoyed.

"But, Mom," she says. "It's true."

"That's enough, Jen," says Big Ears. "Andy wants to know what sort of boy he *really* is. And we're going to help him remember."

"Yes, please," I say, "tell me!"

"Well," says the mother, "you're very helpful. In fact, you're never happier than when you're helping others."

"I am?"

"Yes," says the mother. "You just love housework."

"I do?" I say.

"But not just housework," says Big Ears. "You love working in the yard as well."

"Really?" I say.

"And you love being my slave and doing everything I tell you to do," says the girl.

"I do?" I say.

"Yes!" they say.

The mother hands me a pair of rubber gloves and a bottle of dish soap. "The sooner you get started," she says, "the sooner you'll get your memory back."

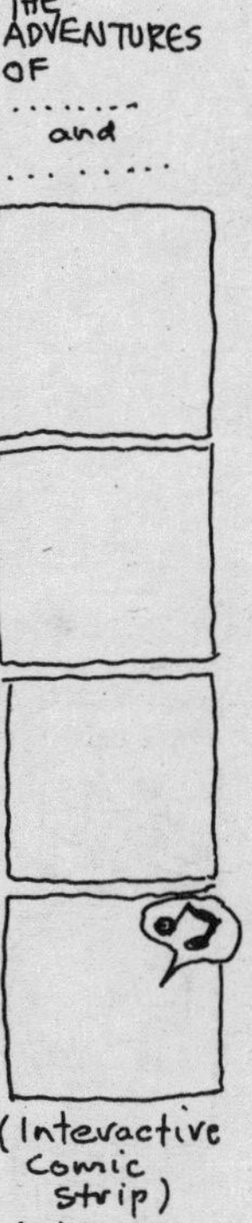

It's 6 P.M. I've washed the dishes, mopped the floor, cleaned the cars, mowed the lawn, cleaned out the gutters, vacuumed every room in the house, cut the girl's toenails, and sorted her CD collection into alphabetical order, but nothing has worked. I still don't know who I am. All I know is I'm exhausted.

Big Ears walks across the backyard toward me.

He is holding a box of cookies and an enor-

mous metal spring with a doll's head jammed on one end. "I assume this is yours," he says.

It looks vaguely familiar.

"It might be," I say. "What is it?"

"I'm not sure," says Big Ears. "Looks like some sort of homemade jack-in-the-box."

Ah! This must be the one that boy was talking about.

Big Ears forces the spring with the doll's head on it down into the box and pushes the lid into place.

He tilts the box toward me.

"Would you like a cookie?" he says.

I hear someone calling out behind me.

I turn around. It's the boy called Danny.

"Hey, Andy!" he says. "Feeling better?"

"Not really," I say.

But the boy's not looking at me or listening to me. He's just staring at the box.

"Don't open that, Mr. G," he says. "It's dangerous!"

Too late. It's open. Everything goes into slow motion. The lid of the box shoots off and whizzes past my ear. The doll's head comes off the spring and hits me right in the middle of my forehead. The spring goes straight up and hits Big Ears in the face.

Everything comes flooding back.

I remember who I am.

I'm Andy. I don't like doing housework or working in the yard. I don't like being Jen's slave. I don't like helping people. I like annoying them. I like playing tricks on them. I am stupid. And I love it.

I hear a moan behind me. I look over.

It's Danny.

He is lying in the driveway. The lid of the cookie box is on the ground beside him.

I run across to him.

"Danny," I say. "Are you okay?"

He rolls his head from side to side and looks at me with a confused cross-eyed stare.

"Danny," he says. "Who's Danny?"

"Dad!" I call. "Help me! Danny's been hurt."

But Dad doesn't answer.

I look around.

He is standing in the middle of the yard, his face in his hands.

"Dad!" I call. "Talk to me!"

He takes his hands away from his face. He looks at me and frowns.

"Dad?" he says. "Who's Dad?"

Dum-Dum

I'm drawing an invisible line down the middle of the table.

"Cross that line and you're dead meat," I say.

Danny puts his finger over the line.

"You mean this line?" he says.

I whack my ruler down the line. He's too slow. The tip nicks his finger.

"Ow!" screams Danny.

"I'm sorry," I say, "but I did warn you."

Mr. Dobson turns around from the board. He is glaring at me.

"Please stand up, Andy," he says.

"But . . ."

"*Stand* up," he says.

I stand up.

More snails on p. 115 → this way →

"Would you mind telling me what just happened?" says Mr. Dobson.

"Nothing, sir," I say.

"Then what was that noise?" says Mr. Dobson. "And why is Danny bent over holding his finger?"

"It's his own fault," I say. "He crossed the line."

"What line?" says Mr. Dobson.

"The line I drew down the middle of the table."

"Andy," sighs Mr. Dobson, "you are acting like a child."

"I am a child, sir," I remind him.

"Are you trying to be funny?" says Mr. Dobson.

"No, sir," I say. "It's a fact."

Sometimes I wonder about Mr. Dobson. Does he think I'd be sitting here if I wasn't a child? I don't see too many adults sitting in on his math classes for the fun of it. Not that I would ever point this out to him. I wouldn't want to hurt his feelings. He probably thinks his math classes are the best entertainment value around.

"Facts?" he says. "You want facts? I'll give you a fact. The fact is that your behavior is lit-

HISTORY OF THE RULER

Young King Arthur tries to pull the ruler from the Rock.

Attila the Hun prepares four battle.

Joan of Arc grasps her 1-foot wooden ruler as she leads the French into battle.

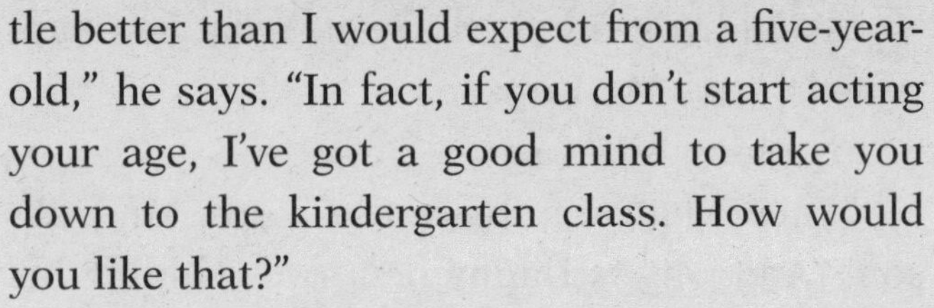

tle better than I would expect from a five-year-old," he says. "In fact, if you don't start acting your age, I've got a good mind to take you down to the kindergarten class. How would you like that?"

"But the line was very clearly drawn," I say. "And I did warn him."

Mr. Dobson just looks at me. He's frowning. I don't think he understands how important invisible lines are in maintaining order in the classroom. The truth is that Mr. Dobson should thank me for helping him keep control of the class, because he certainly can't. Mr. Dobson is our substitute teacher, but if you ask me, he's no substitute for Ms. Livingstone. She's been away for the last two months climbing Mount Everest. I wish she'd hurry up and get back.

Mr. Dobson walks up to my table.

"Come on," he says.

"Where are we going?" I say.

"The kindergarten class," he says. "I've had enough."

Nobody dares to laugh. It's not the first time he's threatened to send somebody to the kindergarten class, but it's the first time he's actually done anything about it.

I pick up my books and pencil case.

ANSWER TO AMAZING EYE TRICK #27 see Pg 42.

As Buddha once read on a Cornflakes box: "To define is to limit." So the answer to this puzzle is: As many differences as you think there ought to be.

Ms. Livingstone I presume.

"Leave your books," says Mr. Dobson. "You won't be needing them."

Of course! Going to kindergarten might not be such a bad thing after all. It will be easier — and a whole lot more fun — than math class. I mean, how hard can some cutting, pasting, and coloring be?

I follow Mr. Dobson out the door.

"So long, suckers," I say over my shoulder to the rest of the class.

I follow Mr. Dobson down the corridor and across the school yard to the elementary school.

"Wait out here," says Mr. Dobson at the entrance to the elementary school building.

He walks down the corridor and knocks on a brightly colored door.

A friendly looking woman wearing a long dress with red flowers all over it opens the door. Mr. Dobson talks to her in a low voice. The woman nods and smiles.

Mr. Dobson motions to me to come closer.

The woman gives me a very sweet smile. She crouches down slightly so we can see eye to eye.

"Hello, Andy," she says. "My name is Mrs. Baxter. Welcome to kindergarten. You're just in time for show-and-tell."

This drawing escaped from: "The Adventures of Balloon Boy" by Jill Groves.

I catch a glimpse over her shoulder of all the kids sitting cross-legged on the floor.

"Cool," I say.

Mrs. Baxter nods at Mr. Dobson.

He nods back.

"Behave yourself, Andy," he says, and walks off up the corridor.

I walk into the room.

All the kindergartners stare.

Mrs. Baxter closes the door behind me and puts her arm around my shoulder.

"This is Andy, everybody," she says. "I'd like you all to make him feel welcome."

"But he's a big kid," says one boy. "He's not a kindergartner."

"But he's welcome all the same," says Mrs. Baxter. "Sit down, Andy."

I stick out my tongue at the kid while Mrs. Baxter's not looking.

"He stuck out his tongue at me," says the kid.

"I did not," I say. "I was licking my lips."

Mrs. Baxter holds up her hands.

"I'm not interested in your stories, Bradley," she says.

"But he did," says Bradley.

"Did not," I say.

"Andy! Please!" says Mrs. Baxter.

I sit down on one of the tiny tables.

Mrs. Baxter shakes her head.

"No, Andy," she says, pointing to the floor.

She wants me to sit cross-legged? On the floor?

"But . . ." I say. "I'm too big to . . ."

"You're part of the group," says Mrs. Baxter. "Just like everybody else."

I don't mind spending a day with the kindergartners, but being made to sit on the floor is going a little too far.

I look for a spot with the boys, but there are no free spaces. I have to sit between two girls.

"All right," says Mrs. Baxter. "Now, where were we?"

"It was my turn," says Bradley.

"Oh, that's right," says Mrs. Baxter. "What would you like to tell us about, Bradley?"

Bradley stands up.

"My grandma," he says.

"And what would you like to tell us about your grandma, Bradley?"

"I don't like her," he says. "She smells funny."

All the kids laugh.

"You smell funny," whispers the girl on my right. She pinches her nose.

"Oh, yeah?" I say. "Well, you smell funny, too."

The girl starts crying.

"Mrs. Baxter," says the girl next to her. "Wendy's crying."

"What's the matter, Wendy?" says Mrs. Baxter.

"He said I stink," she blubbers, pointing at me.

"Is that true, Andy?" says Mrs. Baxter.

"No," I say. "That's not what I said."

"What did you say?" says Mrs. Baxter.

"I said she smelled funny," I say. "But she said it to me first."

"Two wrongs don't make a right," says Mrs. Baxter. "You should know that."

"I know," I say, "but . . ."

"I think you owe Wendy an apology," says Mrs. Baxter.

"But . . ."

"Apologize!" says Mrs. Baxter, flashing me an ice-cold stare.

"I'm sorry I hurt your feelings, Wendy," I say.

She sniffles.

"Good boy, Andy," says Mrs. Baxter, all

sweetness and light again. "That wasn't so hard, was it? Now perhaps you've got something you'd like to share with us for show-and-tell?"

Talk about being put on the spot. I put my hand into my pocket. All I have is my handkerchief, and judging by its hardness, it hasn't been washed in a while. It wouldn't be a pretty sight. I pull out my hand.

"No, Mrs. Baxter," I say. "I don't have anything. Well, nothing you'd want to see, anyway."

"Of course we would, Andy," says Mrs. Baxter. "Don't be shy."

"I'm not being shy," I say. "I just don't have anything to show."

Mrs. Baxter flashes me the icy stare again.

"I think you do," she says.

"Okay," I say. "But don't say I didn't warn you."

I stand up and pull out my handkerchief. It's molded into a hard, crusty ball. It makes a cracking sound as I unfold it. I hold it up in front of my chest.

The kids screw up their faces and groan. Wendy looks like she is going to cry again.

"Ooooh — yuck," says Bradley. "Yuck! Yuck! Yuck!"

"Yuck! Yuck! Yuck!" the kindergartners chant. "Yuck! Yuck! Yuck!"

"Quiet please, everyone," commands Mrs. Baxter. They stop chanting.

She turns to me.

"Put it away now, Andy," says Mrs. Baxter. "It's not funny. Nobody wants to see that."

Well, I did try to warn her. I crush it back up into a ball and sit down.

"All right, show-and-tell is over," says Mrs. Baxter, obviously ready to move on. "Everybody please go to their tables." She looks at me. "You can sit here today, Andy," says Mrs. Baxter, pointing to a seat next to Bradley.

"Why does he have to sit next to me?" says Bradley.

"Because I know you'll look after him," she says.

I sit down. I feel ridiculous in this tiny chair at this tiny table. My knees don't even fit underneath it. Bradley runs his finger down the center.

"Cross this line and you're dead meat," he whispers.

"Grow up," I whisper back.

"All right class," says Mrs. Baxter, "we're going to sing the alphabet. One, two, three."

The class starts up a monotonous chant.

"A . . . B . . . C . . . D . . . E . . . F . . . G . . ."

I chant along with the rest of the kids. This is more like it. This is the sort of easy work I came for. Bradley's chanting is the loudest.

"H . . . I . . . J . . . K . . . ENNEL-MENNEL-BEE . . ." he sings.

"What did you say?" I ask him.

"Ennel-mennel-bee," he says.

"It's not ennel-mennel-bee," I say.

"Yes it is," he says. "That's the words."

"It's L M N O P," I say. "It just sounds like ennel-mennel-bee when you say it fast."

"No it's not, you dum-dum," says Bradley.

"Don't call me a dum-dum, you little shrimp!" I hiss back.

All of a sudden, he comes at me. He knocks me out of my seat. I can't believe it. I'm fighting with a kindergartner. And even worse, he seems to be winning. Somehow he manages to get to a sitting position on top of my chest. He's about to punch me in the nose when Mrs. Baxter grabs his hand.

"Stop it, you two!" she says. "Andy! You should be ashamed of yourself!"

"Me? What about him?" I say. "He started it."

BRADLEY'S ALPHABET.

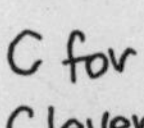

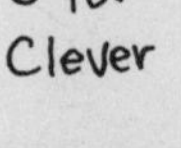

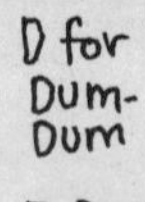

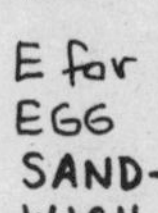

Mrs. Baxter is restraining Bradley. He is like a little wild animal. Snorting and hissing and kicking.

"Bradley is only young," she says. "You're old enough to know better. Get back in your seat."

The rest of the class is whispering and pointing.

This is so unfair. I feel like crying.

"Maybe you're not ready for whole group work yet," says Mrs. Baxter. "Why don't you try doing these by yourself?"

She puts a pile of "Spot the Difference" cards in front of me.

"There are four pictures on each card," she says. "Three are the same. One is different. See if you can tell which is the odd one out."

I look at the cards. The top one has four airplanes on it. I know one is supposed to be different, but as far as I can see, they are all the same.

The rest of the class goes on chanting the alphabet. Every time they come to "L M N O P" Bradley leans toward me and whispers "ennel-mennel-bee" really loudly in my ear. He's making it very hard for me to concentrate on my cards.

I'm still trying to figure out which plane is the odd one when the bell rings for recess. I get up to go.

"Hang on, Andy," says Mrs. Baxter. "Not so fast. Have you finished?"

"Yes," I say. "They're all the same."

"Are you sure about that?" she says.

I look again. The same four planes. All red. All with a little blue circle on the wings.

"Yes," I say. "The same."

"What about that one?" she says, pointing to the plane in the bottom right-hand corner. "Is it going the same way as the others?"

I can't believe it. It's going a different way!

"But how . . . when . . . why . . . ?" I stammer. "It wasn't like that before. . . ."

"Hmmm," says Mrs. Baxter, making a mark in her notebook. "Looks like another area to work on. Run along now and get some fresh air."

I go out of the building and am about to cross the school yard back to the middle school when Mrs. Baxter calls after me.

"Andy! Where do you think you're going?"

"Back to the middle school, Mrs. Baxter," I say.

"No, Andy, that's not allowed," she says.

"Kindergartners have to stay in the area between the building and the big tree."

"But I'm hungry," I say. "I have to get something to eat."

"Sorry, Andy," she says. "But you should have thought about that before you came here."

I look over at the middle school. All my friends are there. Danny and Lisa are sitting next to each other. Lisa has a bag of chips, and Danny is shoving a slice of pie into his mouth.

I can't stand it.

I turn around and go and sit under the big tree with the kindergartners. They are all eating, too. Cookies, string cheese, granola bars, doughnuts — you name it, they've got it. Bradley is eating an enormous piece of chocolate cake. It's almost bigger than his head. And he's got a pretty big head.

"You're not going to eat all of that, are you?" I say.

"Probably not," he says.

"Can I have some?" I say.

"If you can run fast enough," he says. He throws it into the middle of the school yard.

I run to pick it up. I'm just about to grab what's left of the cake when the dog that hangs

around the school yard comes out of nowhere and wolfs it down. I feel like I'm going to cry again.

The bell rings, and we all go back inside.

In the classroom, there are counting blocks laid out on a table. There are two different types of blocks — elephant blocks and chicken blocks.

"Now it's time for math," says Mrs. Baxter. "I have two elephant blocks and three chicken blocks. If I take one elephant away, what do I have left?"

Oh, that's so easy! I put up my hand but Bradley beats me to it.

"One elephant and three chickens," he says.

"Very good," says Mrs. Baxter. "And if I take one chicken away, how many do I have left?"

Easy again! I shoot my hand up.

"Andy?" says Mrs. Baxter.

"One elephant and no chickens," I say.

"Don't you mean one elephant and two chickens?" she says.

"No," I say. "You might think you would have two chickens left, but it's a little trickier than that. See, even if you took only one chicken away, you'd still end up with no chick-

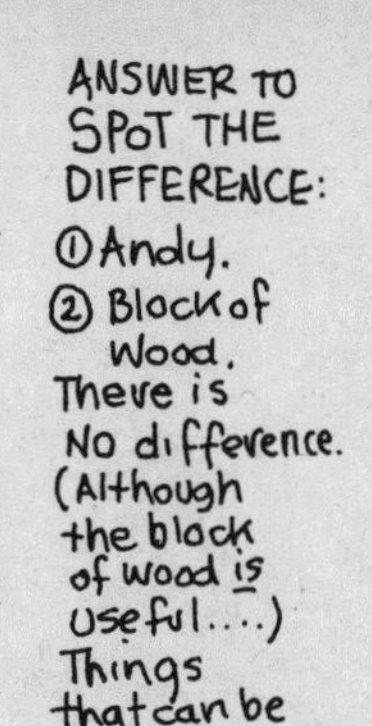

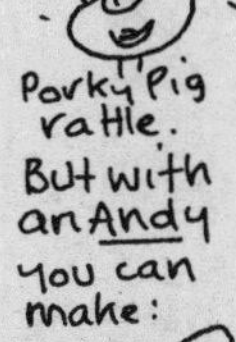

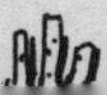

ens because the elephants would stomp on them."

"I don't think you quite understand, Andy," says Mrs. Baxter, making another note in her book. "We're not talking about real elephants and real chickens. These are just counting blocks."

Everybody laughs. I hate kindergartners.

After a little more counting, it's time for art.

We have to draw a picture of our house and family. Now this is something I *can* do.

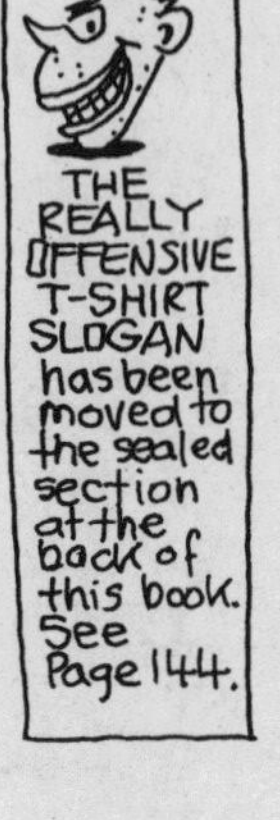

I look across at Bradley's picture. It's really bad. Crooked walls. Stupid colors. The sky is green, the people are all the wrong size and shape, and he's even got a purple dog flying around in the sky. I could do a better drawing than that with my eyes shut, but I'm not going to take any chances. I'm going to do something really impressive.

I use my ruler to draw the sides of my house so that they are really straight. I draw a perfectly pointed roof with a chimney sticking out of the side. I draw a little curly wisp of gray smoke coming out of the chimney and color the sky blue, the grass green, and the sun yellow. It's the best drawing I've ever done. Good enough to hang in an art gallery, I think.

"Mrs. Baxter," calls Bradley. "Andy's copying me."

"I am not," I say.

"Are, too," he says.

"That will do," says Mrs. Baxter. "Copying somebody else's work is very naughty, Andy."

"I wasn't copying," I say.

"He was," says Bradley.

Mrs. Baxter picks up the two drawings and studies them. They look nothing like each other. Anyone can see that.

"See?" I say. "I didn't copy his."

"No," says Mrs. Baxter. "You're right. You didn't copy. Your picture is very different from Bradley's."

"Yeah," I say. "He's got stupid purple dogs flying around a green sky. And his walls are crooked! Look how straight mine are! And everything is the right color. Mine is much better than Bradley's."

"Both of your pictures are very good," says Mrs. Baxter. "Bradley's picture may not be strictly realistic, Andy, but it's very creative. You could learn a lot from Bradley. Try to work more from your heart and less from your head."

I feel like crying again. But this time, I

don't just feel like crying. I actually burst into tears.

ANDY AFTER ONE DAY OF KINDERGARTEN.

Mrs. Baxter puts her arm around me.

"You didn't get off to a very good start today, did you?" she says. "Maybe you'll do better tomorrow."

"I won't be here tomorrow," I say. "I'm just here for the day."

Mrs. Baxter looks concerned.

"The day?" she says. "Mr. Dobson didn't say anything about this being just for the day. He said I was to keep you here until you were ready to go back up. And, quite frankly, Andy, I just don't think you are ready yet. In fact, I'm not sure how you got up there in the first place."

"But . . . but . . . but . . ." I blubber.

"Now come on, Andy," she says. "Cheer up. If you apply yourself and work really hard, you'll be back up with the big children before you know it. And, meanwhile, I'm sure Bradley will enjoy looking after you and being your special friend. Won't you, Bradley?"

Bradley nods.

"Yes, Mrs. Baxter," he says. "I'll look after him."

I'M JUST STUPID.

I look around at all the colorful posters on

the walls and the cheerful decorations. There's a big pink octopus in the corner and two teddy bears in a hot-air balloon hanging from the ceiling. And at the side of the room, there's even a little hook with my name on it. I guess there are plenty of worse places I could be.

I sit down. I wait until Mrs. Baxter's back is turned, and I draw a line down the center of the table.

I grab Bradley by the collar.

"Cross that line and you're dead meat," I say.

He nods.

There are going to be a few changes around here.

Chubby Bunnies

It's Lisa Mackney's birthday party. Lisa and all the girls are in the corner of the room looking at her presents. Danny and I are standing at the food table staring at the biggest bowl of marshmallows we have ever seen.

"Bet I can fit more marshmallows in my mouth than you can," says Danny.

"Bet you can't," I say.

"Wanna make a million-dollar bet?"

"No," I say.

"Why not?" says Danny, looking disappointed.

"You haven't got a million dollars."

"I don't need a million dollars," he says. "Because I'm going to win."

"As if!" I say.

"Am, too," says Danny.

"Are not," I say.

"So, are you in?" says Danny.

"No way," I say.

"Suit yourself," says Danny. "You're out!"

"But I wasn't in!"

"All right," says Danny, "if you're going to whine about it, then you're in — but I'm warning you, you're testing my patience."

He picks up a marshmallow from the bowl.

"Danny!" I say. "For the last time, I'm not playing Chubby Bunnies."

Danny's face drops.

"You're just trying to act mature in front of Lisa," he says.

"Am not," I say. But he's right. I've been trying very hard to be mature and grown-up since I ended up in my underpants in front of her at the school dance. It's been going pretty well, too. Not that she's talked to me that much, but she did invite me to her party, which is a good sign.

"Know what else I think?" says Danny.

"What?" I say.

"You're a wuss."

"Am not," I say.

"Wussy boy, wussy boy," chants Danny. "Andy's a wussy boy."

"Quit it," I say.

But Danny doesn't let up. He's getting louder and louder. There's only one way to stop him.

I take a marshmallow from the bowl and put it in my mouth.

"One Chubby Bunny," I say.

Danny looks me in the eye and smiles. He takes two marshmallows from the bowl and puts them both in his mouth.

"Two Chubby Bunnies," he says.

It's on.

I take two marshmallows from the bowl and put them in my mouth. The marshmallows are making my mouth water, but there's no way I'm going to swallow them. I can't afford for Danny to start singing the wussy boy song again. Lisa might hear him.

"Three Chubby Bunnies," I say.

"Four Chubby Bunnies," says Danny.

I look across at Lisa and the other girls. They are busy with the book I gave Lisa for her birthday. It's called *How To Find Your Perfect Partner Through Palm Reading*.

It's not a very good book because when I

OUT OF MARSHMALLOWS? TRY:
BOLTS.
HOUSE BRICKS.
SMALL FLUFFY DOGS.

checked my palm against the picture of the perfect lover's palm, it looked nothing like it. It does now, though. I fixed the picture up with a black pen. When Lisa comes to check my palm — which I know she will because girls are very curious about that sort of stuff — she's going to discover that I'm her perfect partner!

But first I have to shut Danny up.

"Come on," he says. "Your turn!"

I put two marshmallows in my mouth.

"Five Chubby Bunnies."

It's getting very hard to say "Chubby Bunnies," but then that *is* the point of the game.

Danny picks up a handful of marshmallows. He counts them and stuffs them all into his mouth.

"Ten Chubby Bunnies!" he says, although it sounds more like "dem dubby unnees."

I take an even bigger handful. I poke them one by one into the corners of my mouth. Way down into the bottom of my cheeks. One by one into the space between my gums and the top of my lips. I flatten them and paste them across the roof of my mouth. One underneath my tongue. Others molded around my teeth.

"Fifteen Chubby Bunnies!" I say. Only it

doesn't sound like that. It doesn't sound like anything . . . well, nothing human, anyway.

I've got to admit that I'm feeling pretty proud of myself.

Greg Box likes to stuff his ear full of ibis.

Danny's eyes are wide. He's wondering how he's ever going to top my effort.

Somebody taps me on the shoulder and I almost swallow them all. That was close.

I turn around.

It's Lisa and Roseanne. Lisa is clutching her book.

"Hi, Andy," says Lisa. "Are you having a good time?"

Benny Mussolini likes to see how many pencils he can fit into the holes in his head.

Why does she have to pick now to start talking to me? Right now, when I've got fifteen marshmallows in my mouth? I can't talk to her because I would have to swallow them — and I can't swallow them because I'll lose the competition and owe Danny a million dollars. But I can't not talk to her because, well, she's the most beautiful girl I've ever met. And I can't let her find out that I've stuffed my mouth full of marshmallows because then the most beautiful girl I've ever met will think I'm more of an idiot than she already does.

I do the only thing possible.

I nod.

Pretty rude to just nod when somebody asks you if you're having a good time, I know, but maybe she'll think I'm just the strong silent type.

Palm Reading

She smiles.

"That's good," she says. "Have you had something to eat?"

If only she knew the truth.

I nod again.

Lisa frowns.

"Are you all right?" she says.

I nod for a third time. I give her a thumbs-up and try to smile appreciatively without letting the fifteen marshmallows erupt from my mouth.

Enya O'Brian swallows butterflies.

"Can I ask you something?" she says.

An idea comes to me.

I can't swallow the marshmallows, but maybe I can take them out for a while. We can resume the game later.

I pretend that I'm going to sneeze.

"Ah . . . ah . . ."

I turn away from the table.

"Choo!"

I "sneeze" the marshmallows into my right

hand, wipe my mouth, and turn back to face Lisa and Roseanne.

"Bless you," says Lisa.

"Thanks," I say. "What did you want to ask me?"

She blushes and looks shy.

"Can we see your palm?" she asks.

"Sure," I say.

I hold out my left hand.

She shakes her head.

"No, I need your right hand," she says.

I can feel the wet stickiness of the fifteen half-chewed marshmallows dripping through my fingers. It's not a nice feeling. I don't think Lisa really needs to see this.

"You don't want to see my right hand," I say.

"Yes, I do," she says. "The book says that the right hand gives a more accurate reading."

"Not in my case," I say. "My left hand is much better. Isn't it, Danny?"

He nods. It's not like he can really do anything else.

"Andy," says Roseanne, "just show us your right hand."

I'm going to have to show them my hand.

But not with the marshmallows.

I turn away from them, slip the gooey mess into my jacket pocket, and wipe my palm on my jeans. I hold it out flat.

"Thank you, Andy," says Lisa.

She takes hold of my hand. It is still moist and sticky from the marshmallows, but she doesn't seem to notice. She's too busy comparing it with the picture in her book.

"Good heart line," says Lisa to Roseanne.

"Strong life line," says Roseanne to Lisa.

Wayne Grotzki tries out his new handset.

"This is very promising," says Lisa. She gives me the most beautiful smile and lets go of my hand. She's obviously noticed the similarity between my palm and the picture in the book. Funny about that.

Lisa and Roseanne rush back to the other girls.

Danny shakes me. He points at his mouth.

He points at my pocket. He points at my mouth. He wants to get on with the game.

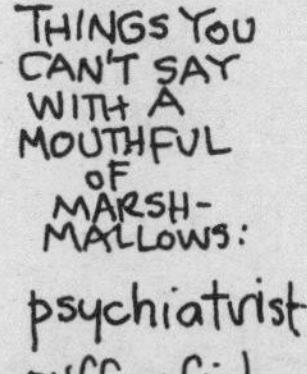

"Okay, okay," I say.

I take the molten mass out of my pocket. It's not quite as white as it was before — there's blue lint and bits of sand embedded in it. But unappealing as it is, I have to put it back in my mouth — the thought of owing Danny a million dollars is much worse.

I cup my hand over my mouth and suck the marshmallows back in. It makes me want to puke, but I stifle the urge.

Danny is holding up six marshmallows. If he can put all of them in his mouth he will be one ahead of me. He pushes them in with ease. The interruption has given him an advantage. His marshmallows have melted more than mine. But that's fair. It was me who stopped.

"Thithsteen thubba ummees," he says, white juice spilling out of the corners of his mouth.

I take another two marshmallows and squash them in my palm to make them as small as possible. I poke them into my bulging mouth.

"Thebentee ubby ubbas," I say.

Seventeen! This must be a world record. Danny will never beat this.

But he pushes another one into his mouth. And another. And another. And another. That's twenty! That's incredible. But I'm not through yet.

I push one in. My bottom jaw feels like it's going to come apart from my top jaw.

I push another one in. My head is going to explode. My eyeballs are going to pop out.

I push the twentieth marshmallow in. It pops straight back out. I pick it up and use the straw from my drink to push it as far into my mouth as I can.

I've done it! We're even! I'm about to try for twenty-one when I feel another tap on my shoulder.

"Andy?"

I turn around.

It's Lisa again. With her book.

"Sorry," she says. "I just need to check your mount of Venus."

She grabs my hand and pokes the fleshy part at the base of my thumb.

She looks back across to the girls.

"It's true!" she calls. "It's true!"

The girls all come running over.

Lisa displays my hand to them.

"See?" she says, holding up the picture in the book as well. "The same!"

"Let's have a look at his other hand!" says Roseanne.

She grabs my left hand.

"A perfect match!" she announces.

Lisa beams.

I can't believe how well she's fallen for my trick. I only wish I didn't have twenty marsh-

mallows in my mouth. I think I'd be as happy as she is.

"You have to kiss now," says Roseanne. "Come on, Andy. Kiss Lisa!"

Somebody throws a handful of glitter over us.

"Lovers!" they cry.

Lisa closes her eyes and puts her cheek forward. It is the most beautiful cheek I have ever seen. It is like the cheek of a princess in a fairy tale. It is a lovely pink color, and the glitter is making it sparkle.

I want to kiss her.

I really do.

But I can't.

What I really want to do is sneeze. For real this time. I think some glitter has gone up my nose. And when you're holding twenty marshmallows in your mouth and you're standing in front of the most beautiful girl in the universe, that's a problem.

I've got to swallow.

I've got to swallow before I sneeze.

But I can't. It's like trying to swallow a wet washcloth. I've simply got too much in my mouth.

I try to turn away and put my hands over

my mouth like when I did the fake sneeze, but I can't. Lisa's holding my right hand. Roseanne is holding my left.

"Ah . . . ah . . ."

There's no stopping it. I wrench my left hand away from Roseanne and try to put it across my mouth in time.

"Choo!"

Too late.

The marshmallow mush comes leaping through my fingers. It's like the white foam on the edge of a breaking wave.

"He's frothing at the mouth!" screams Roseanne. "He's got rabies!"

The remains of twenty half-chewed marshmallows have gone all over the front of my shirt, my jeans, my shoes, and the carpet.

At least they didn't go all over Lisa.

Correction.

At least most of them didn't go all over Lisa. She hasn't noticed yet, but a glob of marshmallow goo has landed right in the middle of her cheek. It looks a lot like — well, I won't say — but it comes out the back end of birds.

Everybody is staring at me.

"You poor thing," says Lisa, rubbing my back. "Are you feeling okay?"

Hey! She thinks I'm sick! Maybe this is not so bad after all.

I bend over and groan.

"Must have been a bad marshmallow," I say.

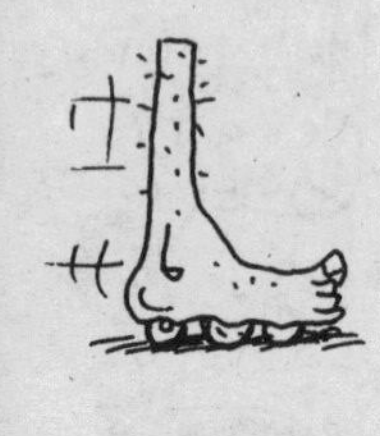

I look up.

Danny is dancing around the room.

"I win!" he cries. "I win!"

Everyone is staring at him.

I'm trying to signal to him to shut up — to let him know that I'll concede victory if only he'll shut up. But he doesn't take the hint.

"What do you mean, Danny?" says Lisa, puzzled.

"You spew, you lose," says Danny. "And he spewed!"

"I did not spew," I say. "I sneezed."

"Same difference," he says. "You owe me a million bucks!"

"What are you talking about?" says Lisa. "What did you win?"

"Chubby Bunnies!" says Danny. "Twenty marshmallows each. But he couldn't hold his!"

As what has happened dawns on everybody, their looks of sympathy turn to disgust.

Danny starts up his victory dance again.

"Twenty marshmallows," he sings. "Twenty marshmallows."

I fold my arms, roll my eyes, and shake my head.

"He is so immature," I say to Lisa.

"He's not the only one," says Lisa.

What can I say? How can I make her understand that I didn't *want* to play Chubby Bunnies? That Danny left me no choice?

"I know what you're thinking . . ." I say.

"You do?" says Lisa, picking up a marshmallow and squeezing it between her thumb and fingers. "What am I thinking?"

"You're thinking that I'm really immature and gross and disgusting. . . ."

"That's right," says Lisa. "But that's not all."

"It's not?"

"No," she says. "I also think you've got a very big mouth."

"Right," I say.

"But not as big as mine," she says.

Lisa puts the marshmallow into her mouth without taking her eyes from mine.

"One Chubby Bunny," she says.

About the Author

Andy Griffiths discovered a talent for being stupid at an early age. Since then, he has amazed the world with a truly stunning array of minor mistakes, major miscalculations, idiotic acts, inane remarks, incomprehensible behavior, and extremely stupid stories. You can find examples of all of these in his other books, including *Just Annoying!*, *Just Joking!*, *The Day My Butt Went Psycho!*, and *Zombie Butts from Uranus!*

About the Illustrator

Terry Denton was born in Venezuela in 1909. He sailed on the maiden voyage of the *Titanic* in 1912 and was lost at sea. He came back to life in 1932, working as an ironing board for Mrs. Ida Bugg of Wisconsin. He would have been the first ironing board to conquer Mt. Everest if it weren't for a nasty bus accident on the way to the airport. Reincarnated (again) in 1963, he worked as a hostess on *Snail of the Century* before retiring to illustrate children's books. In 1985, he gave birth to quintuplets. He now lives a quiet life with his six quintuplets between the covers of this stupid book.